MW01247254

Cobasfang Justice Returns

DAVID WALKER

Copyright © 2018 David Walker
All rights reserved
First Edition

PAGE PUBLISHING, INC.
New York, NY

First originally published by Page Publishing, Inc. 2018

ISBN 978-1-64214-457-4 (Paperback)
ISBN 978-1-64214-456-7 (Digital)

Printed in the United States of America

MY DEDICATION

With my deepest gratitude, from the bottom of my heart, I wish to shout to the world, thank you.

To my family, to the ones that stand by my side when things are uncertain and life has become a struggle. For standing behind me even when the path I am blazing is running in a circle, and for standing in front of me and leading the way when I am overwhelmed and lost my way. But most of all, for giving me the courage to be myself.

To my parents, who were able to raise six kids without losing their minds or one of us in the store (namely, me, running straight for sporting goods and the toy section). Trust me, at one time, they had six teenagers, two dogs, and a whole lot of crazy times bouncing off the walls.

To the Baltimore Science Fiction Society and its insightful observations, I was finally able to polish my dreams and turn them into reality.

Without a doubt, I would like to give *you* my deepest gratitude for taking my dream into your life. Now it's time to let the creatures that filled the halls of my imagination to cross the boundaries of time and space and into your world. Enjoy!

CHAPTER 1

The Journey Begins

From the moment a child is born, their precious life will swing beneath the tender threads of their choices. Most choices are made with little thought or concern while the treacherous ones will twist the reality that binds their fate. Soon, Ty will realize how thin the web is that binds his soul to life when he decides to take matters into his own hands and enter the Forbidden Forest.

To tell you the truth, I am not quite sure where to start. So I guess, since this whole story is about Ty, I'll just take a second to tell you a little bit about him before we begin. So if you are ready, just sit back and relax, but you better hold on tight because that incredible journey one boy went through might change your life too.

His full name is Tyler, but since everybody calls him Ty, we will too. He has deep brown eyes, his hair is kind of short, and he's about your age. Now Ty lives with his mom and dad, grandmother, and his little brother, Bob. He likes to play games with his brother at night and go fishing with his dad whenever he gets a chance. But when he gets out of school, he loves to go out bike riding with his best friends, Dylan and Xavier, or go exploring in the fields on the outskirts of town next to the barricade. But sometimes, when there's nothing to do, Ty will just hang out and read or just play cards in the tree fort.

This wild adventure of Ty started early on a warm and sunny Saturday morning in the beginning of summer. He, Xavier, and Dylan were all sitting inside the tree fort they built at the end of the street behind old man Grady's house. Their fort was really cool; it was made out of old lumber that they scavenged from the lumberyard across town. It had a thick, sturdy door and two windows made from the doors off an old washer and dryer. Its roof was made out of an old blue tarp that would flap when the wind blew hard through the tree. They had a table and three old folding chairs, but one of the coolest things this fort had was a secret trapdoor hidden beneath a rug under a rope hammock in the corner.

Now Ty, Xavier, and Dylan were all sitting inside playing cards when Bob came bursting up through the trapdoor, crying and yelling his head off for Ty.

"What your problem, Bob?" Ty snapped. "You know you can't come in until you knock!"

"Ty, I think Dad's hurt! I just saw Uncle John carrying Dad down the street headed back home. C'mon, Ty. Let's go."

"What do you mean Dad's hurt? Just go back home and I'll be right behind you."

Just as Bob slipped back through the trapdoor, Dylan looked out the window. "I don't see them. Do you want us to go with you, Ty?"

"No, I don't know. Guys, I've gotta go. But I'll meet you at the pond after dinner if you want to go fishing."

Ty tossed his cards on the table, then slipped out through the trapdoor and scurried down the tree, but when he ran around old man Grady's pool, he saw Bob in the front yard, pinned against a big tree by the neighborhood bullies, Pete and Joe. Those two jerks were two years older and a lot bigger than Ty and always in trouble. Every time something went wrong or someone got in trouble, you always heard their names shouted out first. They had Bob pinned against that tree real hard and were shoving a long black snake in Bob's face, screaming that they were going to shove it down his shirt. Bob was so terrified of snakes he couldn't move an inch.

"Hey! What's going on?" shouted Ty as he ran up to those two bullies. "Leave my brother alone!"

As Ty tried to rip that snake out of Joe's hands, Pete turned around, grabbed him by his shirt, slammed him to the ground, and sat on Ty's chest, screaming, "After we take care of your little brother, you're next!"

Joe still had Bob pinned against that thick tree trunk and was trying to uncoil that snake from around his arm so he could shove it down Bob's shirt.

Ty fought back wildly against Pete. They went rolling across the yard and into the deep, muddy ditch, swinging and punching each other as hard as they could.

All of a sudden, Joe went flying into the ditch, crashing on top of Ty and Pete with a huge thud.

Xavier and Dylan were standing at the top of the ditch with their hands on their hips, looking down as Pete and Joe rolled over onto their backs, trying to figure out what just happened.

"Get out of here right now or we are going to bust you two up!" shouted Dylan.

Pete and Joe knew they were outnumbered, so they took off running down the block, but you could hear Joe screaming back at them, "This ain't over!" as those two ducked around the next house.

"Thanks, guys," Ty gasped as he stood up and brushed the mud off his pants. "Those two are going to get it for messing with my little brother!"

"Are you okay, Bob?" Ty muttered, crawling out of that ditch. "You got to get over being afraid of snakes. They can't hurt you. Now c'mon, let's get back home. OK?"

Ty held Bob's hand as they started running back home, but as soon as they got close to their front yard, Bob took one look at Ty and bolted for the door. Bob was running so fast that he nearly knocked his mom down as she tried to open the door open.

"What happened to you and your brother? You're all muddy, and you're making a mess in my living room," she grumbled.

"Sorry, Mom," Ty said. "We were at the fort playing cards with Dylan and Xavier, and we fell in the ditch walking home by Mister Grady's house. What happened to Dad?"

"Your father got hurt at Eagle Cliff, digging for some blue fire rubies for Grandma. He should know better than that. Those tunnels near the northern cavern are too dangerous and they are unstable, just like your father!"

"Unstable or not, that's where you have to dig. If you had the slightest clue about geology, you would know that!" Ty's dad snapped back. "We had to dig pretty deep through a vein of iron ore when John spotted a small cluster growing out from behind a large chunk of bedrock. We dug as hard as we could when, all of a sudden, the walls started to collapse! Those huge timbers we used to shore up the roof started snapping like toothpicks. John and I barely got out of there with our lives, and just as we dove out of the cave, a timber came hurling out and hit me in the leg. I think it's broke."

"Tyler, go and get my bag from downstairs," Ty's mom said sternly. "And, John, would you go into the kitchen, grab the small blue bowl under the counter, and fill it halfway with soap and water so I can clean this leg off and get a better look? There's a clean washcloth in the drawer next to the sink. Grab one of the green ones, not my good white ones."

Ty's mom just happened to be the best doctor in town, and she knew right away that his dad's leg didn't look too good. She put her coffee down on the end table and then bent down to get a good look. She examined his injured leg very carefully and could see right away that it was broken.

"When you break something, you sure do make a mess of things," she said. "But don't worry, it's going to be really easy to fix your leg. It won't take me long to put a cast on it, but I'm afraid that you're going to have to use crutches for at least six weeks."

"Yeah, I know," he sighed. "But it wasn't a total disaster because, before the cave collapsed, we were able to grab a small chunk from that cluster of rubies. Look, I grabbed three real nice blue fire rubies."

While John cleared off a spot on the table to put the bowl of soapy water down, Ty's mother took a look at what he brought home.

"These are some real nice ones, and they have a real strong glow, but I'm afraid they just won't be enough. They're just too small, "Ty's mom said. "Now If I mix them with some papa root, I think I might be able to make just enough to make Grandma feel a lot better for a couple more days. Honey, I'm going to need a lot more just as strong as these if I'm going to have any chance to cure her."

(I guess I forgot to tell you about blue fire rubies. You see, they get their name because of the warm mystical glow that swirls around them when the light is dim or when a storm approaches. You can tell how old they are by how deep the fire grows when you hold them in your hands. The reason why they are so valuable is that when a true crystal healer makes potions out of them, they can heal all kinds of injuries or even cure diseases. Nowadays, the only place left that you can find these gems is deep inside the caves at Eagle Cliff, and if those old stories are true, you might find some in the caves hidden deep within the Shadow Forest! Nobody really knows for sure because, in the last two hundred years, no one has ever made it out of there alive.)

Just then, Ty ran back upstairs and placed the medical bag on the table next to his mom. "Is Dad going to be okay?" asked Ty.

"He will be fine," his mom replied. "And you get out of those muddy clothes right now. Your sisters, Cristan and Kelly, are coming over to visit later and we'll be eating soon, so if you go anywhere, don't be late or you will miss lunch."

Ty ran upstairs to his room and got changed. Bob was sitting in Ty's room, still shaken up from what those bullies tried to do. Ty sat down next to Bob on the bed and told him, "Don't you worry about those jerks. I'll make sure they never mess with you again!" Bob stood up and threw a pillow across the room, knocking an empty cup off to Ty's dresser, trying to look tough. "I'm not afraid of them. I was just scared that the snake would eat me!"

Ty just smiled. "I'll teach you all about snakes so you will never be scared of them anymore. Okay? Now you tell Mom I am going fishing at the river and I might spend the night at Dylan's house. Oh yeah! Mom said don't forget to wash your hands before you come down."

Ty crawled out the window and headed down his secret trail to the edge of the river. This was where Ty always went when he wanted to do some serious thinking.

As Ty sat down in his favorite spot on the old tree stump next to the great pit, he just leaned back and started to toss a few rocks in. This hidden spot on the river's edge was a forbidden place where Ty and his friends would sometimes go when they got bored. They would throw rocks into the great pit just to see if they could hear one hit the bottom. Last year, Dylan swore that he tossed a huge rock down there and heard a ghostly squeal come up from the depths of that deep, dark hole. Nobody really knew how deep it was because nobody was ever stupid enough to climb down there. Not even Pete and Joe.

While he sat there, Ty just couldn't stop thinking about what his mom had said about his grandma, and he knew that his dad wouldn't be able to get any more healing rubies now that he had a broken leg. Ty wanted to do something to help save his grandma, and since his dad couldn't do anything with a broken leg, he figured it would be up to him to find some more blue fire rubies.

With the caves by Eagle Cliff destroyed, the only other place to find the rubies would be deep within the Shadow Forest. However, the thought of going in that place scared him so much that he nearly threw up. Ty knew that the creatures that lurked in the Shadow Forest were ten times worse than any nightmare you could ever have. It was said that there were mystical witches so powerful that they could capture you in a blink of an eye and feast on your bones for a hundred years. Sometimes at night, when the air was calm and the night mist crawled across the ground, Ty and Bob would crawl out of their window, sit on the edge of their roof, and listen to their nightmarish howling echoing out from the depths of those forbidden woods.

This is the reason why the grown-ups where Ty lives surrounded their town with huge rows of razor bushes. Now everybody knows that razor bushes are nothing to mess with. Their silvery leaves are about the size of a bottle cap and are sharper than any razor blade ever made. Sometimes, in the cool dim light of the moons, Ty could see the leaves shimmering with an eerie green glow from his bedroom window. Those razor bushes are the perfect thing to protect the town from the nightmarish creatures that creep in those woods. Just the slightest brush against the smallest leaf will slice even the toughest monster to the bone.

All Ty could think about was how badly his grandmother needed those blue fire rubies. He knew that if his mom found out what he was planning to do, she would lock him up in his room and never let him out again. He stood up slowly and looked over to the edge of the shadow forest and took a deep breath. Ty knew that if he was going to do this, he would have to go now. He realized that if he went home and grabbed the things he would need, his mom would figure out what he was planning to do in a second and stop him cold.

Ty just stood there for a moment and started to smile a sneaky, sinister little smile and thought, *No problem*. He brushed the dirt off his pants and figured he might as well get started. Then with a deep breath, he gathered up some courage and boldly started walking across the field, heading straight for the Shadow Forest. The grass was swaying back and forth as a bone-chilling wind swept down from the mountain. *This is not a good sign*, Ty thought, but he just clenched his teeth and kept on walking. As he got closer to the edge of the forest, a ghostly mist started to rise up from the ground and swept across his feet. Ty stopped right there, realizing there was absolutely no way he was going to go in there unarmed. So he started looking around to see what kind of weapon he could come up with as he walked down the trail. Now Ty was a smart kid, but there was nothing in that field at all, except for some rocks and grass.

Wait just a minute, Ty thought. *This might work quite nicely.*

Ty reached down and picked up a couple of flat skipping stones from the side of the trail and started chipping away at the sides of those rocks just like the great Indians used to do. Before long, he had made himself a very sharp stone knife and some real cool arrowheads. The moment Ty got to the edge of the forest, he grabbed the straightest and strongest stick he could find to make himself a spear! Next, he used the cord from his jacket hood and a sturdy branch from a hickory tree to make an extra strong bow. With arrows made from solid oak and razor-sharp arrowheads of stone, he was ready to enter those dangerous woods.

O' course, Ty was still a bit scared, but who could blame him? He was alone in the Shadow Forest, armed only with a handful of arrows, a spear, and a knife made of stone. Making weapons strong enough to protect himself wasn't the only problem Ty had to solve. The biggest one of all would be making sure he didn't get lost; he had to be super careful if he was going to find his way back. Ty knew he had to get his bearings, but the forest was so thick with trees and bushes he couldn't see very far at all. So he started looking for the tallest tree he could climb to get a good look around. That was when he saw it. Just up ahead on top of the hill was the biggest tree he had ever seen in his life—a massive oak tree growing right out of a huge pile of boulders.

I don't know about you, but I think doing some boulder hopping and climbing trees is almost as much fun as jumping your bike off ramps into Jason's pond, and Ty thought so too.

So Ty took off and started running as fast as he could. In just a couple of minutes, he made it to the edge of the pile of boulders. With one gigantic leap after another, Ty pounced and lunged from one jagged boulder to the next until he reached the base of that mighty oak tree.

Ty looked up at that tree and smiled because it looked like it was going to be a lot of fun to climb. So he jumped up as high as he could, grabbed ahold of the lowest branch, and swung into action. It was a perfect climbing tree! Each branch was so close it was almost like climbing a ladder. Ty was having so much fun hopping from branch to branch he didn't even notice they were starting to pop and creak the higher he climbed. In no time at all, he had to start squirming and wiggling between the branches as he neared the top, and that's when Ty had his first good look at the Shadow Forest below.

It was the most beautiful thing Ty had ever seen. The forest looked like a green wave of trees flowing across the land like an ocean, splashing against the mountains in the distance. As Ty sat there looking at the forest below, he spotted something quite incredible. In the distance, a magnificent mountain sparkled and glittered as if it was made of diamonds. Now that looked like a perfect place to find what he was after.

"This is going to be easier than I thought." Ty chuckled as he started to climb back down.

About halfway down, Ty heard a strange noise coming from the heart of the forest. It was a low rumbling and crushing sound, getting closer and closer. Suddenly, the whole tree started to rock back and forth from the shock waves of those frightening sounds. Ty held his breath, trying as hard as he could not to make a sound, as he strained to see what was coming. It didn't take long before he got a glimpse of something that sent shivers down his back. He couldn't believe his eyes as he watched two huge horn-backed bears burst out of the woods like scared little rabbits. That was when Ty saw what they were so afraid of: it was a gigantic rinog lumbering out of the shadows of the forest and stepping into the clearing

If you never heard of a rinog before, let me tell you. They are the most ferocious creatures alive, and they are known worldwide for being the worst-tempered creature on the planet. As you might imagine, a rinog has a head like a rhino and club-like hands, and their hide's so tough no spear ever made can penetrate it. This huge monster had to be at least ten feet tall from the tip of its huge gray horns to the ground. Ty took one looked at the weapons he had and knew. If that thing saw him, he would be a goner. So he held on to that tree as hard as he could, not moving a muscle.

Ty clung on to that branch as hard as he could and silently prayed that the beast couldn't hear the sound of his heart pounding in his chest. The woods instantly went quiet, the crickets stopped chirping, the birds in the trees slipped silently deeper within their nests as that beast lumbered through the thick, tall grass. The clearing was as quiet as a graveyard on a cold winter's night.

Just when the rinog walked beneath that mighty oak tree, a loud crack rang out from the branch Ty was clinging on to. A bead of sweat rolled down Ty's forehead as he peered down at the top of its head as it stood there grunting at the buzzing flies. The branch he was clinging on to wasn't going to hold much longer. He was in real serious trouble. If that rinog spotted him, it would crush his bones into dust.

With a chilling growl, it looked all around, trying to find out what made the noise. You could see the muscles rippling in its massive body as it scavenged through the boulders, searching for something to crush. Suddenly, it must have seen something lurking in the shadows deep within the woods because it took off running like a demon on fire. The ground shook like thunder as the trees smashed to the ground when it disappeared into the woods. Ty didn't even try to climb down until the ground stopped shaking and the crickets started chirping once again. That was way too close!

Ty leaned back, wiped the sweat from his brow, and finally exhaled. He admitted to himself the cold, hard fact that if he wasn't more careful, he would never make it out of there alive. After sitting quietly for a moment, gathering his nerve, he reached up and grabbed the crooked branch above him to start climbing back down. But before he could get a good hold of it, the branch he was standing on snapped in half, sending Ty tumbling down toward the cold, hard ground.

"Oh no!" screamed Ty.

Smacking and slamming from branch to branch, Ty fell out of control through the tree. He tried as hard as he could to grab ahold of a branch to stop himself, but he was falling way too fast, and he was seconds away from crashing onto the jagged boulders below.

What should I do? he thought in a panic. Then in a frantic move, Ty grabbed his stone knife and slammed it so hard into that tree's leathery trunk that it split open wide and stuck in deep, saving him from splattering against the boulders below!

With his last bit of strength, Ty ripped his knife free and jumped onto the boulders below. He landed really hard on one of the large flat ones then quickly sat down. He was still pretty scared and shaking uncontrollably on top of that cold and slippery boulder. His side was all scraped up and throbbing with pain.

That was way too close! he thought.

But that would be nothing compared to the trouble that lay ahead for our young hunter.

The Vipercon Attacks

After Ty regained his strength, he slowly and carefully headed off toward the Crystal Mountain. Ty figured he should stay close to the trees, just in case that rinog returned. As he limped along the edge of the forest, he couldn't help noticing how the woods smelled kind of musty and stale and the ground was thick with leaves, making it soft and spongy. The woods seemed to be crawling with all kinds of creatures. Everywhere he looked, from every dark crevice, there were eyes watching him. It felt real spooky walking through those woods during the day, and he was afraid to imagine what it going be like when darkness came.

When Ty made it to the bottom of the next ravine, he had an unexpected surprise. It was a large sweet apple tree. *What perfect timing*, he thought. After all that walking, some nice fresh apples would hit the spot. He looked around to make sure the coast was clear, ran up to it, then filled his arms with a dozen plump, delicious apples. He was feeling really proud of himself, making it all this way, and finding food gave him the confidence to keep on going. So he sat down in the cool shade of that apple tree, ate a few apples, and filled his pockets for a snack later.

Ty was desperate to find the hidden caverns in the Shadow Forest so he could get what he came for and get out alive that he quickly jumped up and started to make his way to the Crystal Mountain. Ty walked slowly across the bottom of that ravine, trying not to make a sound as he made his way over loose rocks and rotting logs. But as he approached the other end of the ravine, he started to gag on the awful stench that swept across the ground like a thick green cloud. It was so bad that he covered his mouth with his shirt as his eyes started to water.

Ty took a few minutes to keep from getting sick and then crawled over an old moldy willow tree lying at the edge of the ravine. Up ahead was a disgusting swamp, bubbling with brown slime that exploded in orange flames as it popped on the surface. Now that was the nastiest thing he had ever seen in his life. There was no way on earth he was going to walk through that bubbling pool of sludge. But turning back now was not an option, so Ty had no choice. He had to find a way around that swamp.

Staying as far away from that mushy ground as he could, Ty started climbing through the thick bushes that grew along the side of the hill. As he struggled to make his way past a dead sticker bush, Ty spotted a creepy cave all covered with green moss. *Why not?* Ty thought. *This is as good a place as any to start looking for the blue fire rubies, and if I find some here, I won't have to go any further.*

Ty was well aware of the dangers hidden deep inside of caves, so he held his spear tightly and then walked in nice and slow. The first thing he found was a couple of green vampire bats hanging from the ceiling and all kinds of poisonous spiders crawling around the cold, damp walls. After flicking a couple of the bigger ones out of his way with the tip of his spear, he crouched down lower and kept on going, but there was something about this cave that didn't seem right. As he slowly made his way deeper into that cave, he started to hear the faint sounds of a few stones tumbling down the side of the cave's wall right in front of him. Ty's heart started pounding in his chest. He knew that he wasn't alone.

Suddenly, Ty heard a soft voice whispering from deep from inside the cave. "Don't be afraid. Just come a little closer. You look like a tasty little snack."

Now as you've already seen, Ty was no fool, so he kept his spear ready and backed out of the cave in a hurry. Standing outside, on solid ground again with his spear held ready, Ty shouted as loud as he could, "Those are brave words coming from someone cowering inside a cave. Why don't you come out here and say that to my face if you dare?"

Ty stood there defiantly, staring into the blackness of the cave. "Well? What's wrong? Did you lose your appetite?"

That's when Ty spotted two green eyes as large as dinner plates slowly moving closer and closer to the opening of the cave. Ty took a step back, braced himself, and shouted out defiantly, "I don't know who you are, but if you think you're going to make me your snack, all I can tell you is you're right about to have a real bad day!"

Suddenly, out of the shadows deep within the cave, slithered the biggest vipercon he had ever seen. (You might not know this, but vipercons are the most poisonous snake on the whole planet. If that isn't bad enough, they are famous for having big appetites and bad tempers.) This one looked to be about fifty feet long, with thick black stripes running down its green scaly back. It slowly slithered out into the daylight and coiled up right in front of Ty.

"You look a little puny to have such a big mouth," it hissed. "But I am hungry and you will have to do."

"I don't have time for this foolishness, so you better get back in your hole or I will make snake-skin boots for my whole family out of you!" shouted Ty as he puffed out his chest and slammed the butt of the spear deep into the ground.

"How dare you talk to me that way!" hissed the vipercon.

Quick as lightning, it reached down and snatched Ty right off the ground, wrapped its huge, muscular body tightly around Ty, and then slowly started to squeeze the life out of our young warrior. The more Ty struggled, the tighter that beast squeezed. Within seconds of being snatched up in that vipercon's mighty grip, Ty's legs were starting to go cold and numb.

With a cold and heartless hiss, that vipercon muttered, "If you have anything else to say, you can say it to my stomach." It opened its huge blood-dripping mouth and lunged for the killing strike.

"I don't think so!" Ty shouted out loud and defiantly.

With a flick of his wrist, Ty reached up and grabbed that thing by its fangs and pulled it up close to him so they were nose to nose.

Ty took his spear and stuck it right between those two huge green eyes and said, "Look here, rat breath. You don't know who you're messing with, and I don't have time to teach you some manners, so you better put me down or I'll break this spear off in your head and leave you for the flies and maggots to feast on!"

"You're very brave for such a little thing," it said in a soft and teasing voice, "or very stupid! Either way, you speak with a sharp tongue. I have a sharp tongue too. Let's see how you like how sharp *my* tongue can be."

It flicked its tongue out and—*smack!* It slapped Ty across his face as hard as it could. His head flew back so hard he swore he was hit with a hammer. Ty let out a thunderous roar, shook his head, and slung that vipercon's spit in all directions.

"You disgusting rat-filled worm, that's the grossest thing ever! But if you are really that hungry, why don't you have an apple?" Just as fast as he could, Ty reached into his pocket and pulled out an apple, then stuck it on that vipercon's fang!

"How dare you!" it hissed furiously. "I'll crush you for that!" Then it started to squeeze even harder and harder. So hard, in fact, that Ty thought his bones were starting to crack.

"I warned you, rat breath! It seems like I'm going to have to teach you a lesson." Looking deeply into those cold green eyes, he grabbed that fang, dripping with venom, and ripped it right out of the vipercon's mouth!

"Ouch! That hurts!" it screamed out in shock as it snapped its head back.

Ty shouted back to that slithery giant, "If you want to live, you had better put me down right now before I get really get mad and put that fang back in your head, pointy side first!"

With blood gushing out from its jaw, the vipercon slowly let Ty back to the ground. "You are a very brave creature," it muttered as it spit some blood on the ground. "My name is Normack. Who are you?"

Ty tried as hard as he could to stand up straight, but his legs were numb and nearly crushed. So he stuck his spear into the ground and held on to it tightly. "My name is Ty, and I'm on a journey through these dark woods in search of blue fire rubies. There is a mountain on the other side of this swamp just west of here that sparkles like diamonds. I am headed there to start my search."

"I have been to that place before. It is a dangerous journey indeed. I can take you there safely if you want."

"Oh really?" Ty laughed aloud. "I don't believe you. Do you think I am stupid or something, and why should I trust you? You'll just try to eat me once my back is turned."

The vipercon rose straight up in the air and replied with a thunderous voice, "Are you calling me a liar? If there is one thing about a vipercon you had better understand is that we do not lie. We do not trick or deceive. We are an honorable race, and our word is our bond! No creature has ever stood his ground to me and walked away. I owe you a debt of honor. I will pay this debt to you by helping you find your treasures. I give you my word!"

Ty still thought this could be a trick, but he figured it would be better to travel next to this vipercon than to worry about it sneaking up on him.

"Sure," Ty said. "I would enjoy some company, but if this is some kind of trick and you try to eat me again, you will be sorry you ever came out of your cave!"

"I won't ever try to eat you again, young master," Normack replied. "To tell you the truth, you tasted worse than fish feet rotting in a pool of swamp sludge!"

"Very funny, especially coming from someone whose breath smells like wet rat butt."

They both started to laugh so hard that they couldn't breathe! It looked like Ty had made himself a friend out here in the Shadow Forest.

After Normack stopped laughing, he told Ty, "If you want to go to the Crystal Mountain, then we must cross the swamp. There's a great place, not far up ahead, where we can safely swim across. The muck floating on top is thin and it won't drag you down."

"Are you crazy? You want to swim across this?" Ty laughed. "I wouldn't get in this bubbling sludge even if the woods were on fire. Anyway, I can't swim, so we have to find another way around."

"What do you mean you can't swim?" chuckled Normack. "It's hard to believe how someone that tastes like a rotting fish's corpse can't even swim across one little swamp. Don't worry, I know another way you can get across without getting your scales wet. About ten years ago, a tornado ripped through here like a demon and blew down an enormous willow tree. It was so huge it fell completely across the swamp. You might be able to use it like a bridge. That is, if you have enough balance with those little feet of yours to walk across it."

"All right!" grumbled Ty. "Let's get to the tree as fast as we can because if I have to smell this place any longer, I am going to throw up."

Normack led the way through the thick brush covering the bank of that swamp. Smashing flat the twisted thorn bushes, he made a nice path for Ty to follow. It didn't take long until they made it to the tree bridge. (Let me tell you, it looked more like a floating pile of weeds than a tree.) But Ty knew that it if he didn't cross there, it would take days to walk all the way around that massive swamp.

"I'll go first," Ty said. "But let's go cross one at a time. I don't think this floating flytrap you call a bridge can hold the both of us."

Ty held his breath and cautiously started weaving around the rotting branches, trying desperately not to slip on the slimy wet moss. Every step he took, some gross black goop would start oozing up from what was left of the tree trunk. The further he went out, the deeper the tree started to sink. He could hear it pop and squish as he made his way across, but using his spear to keep his balance, he just kept on going, inch by inch. When he made it to the dead rat that was floating in the bubbling muck, he knew that he was getting closer to the other side. Then all of a sudden, Ty slipped on a slug and started to fall in backwards. In a desperate move, he slammed his spear deep into the tree, jumped back to get his balance, and held on for dear life! But his foot broke through the log and got jammed deep inside, trapping him as the tree started to pitch and roll over.

"Look out, Ty!" yelled Normack as he watched helplessly from the shore.

"No way am I going to fall in this mess!" screamed Ty as held on as tight as he could, bending and twisting his spear, trying desperately to keep from falling in, while the tree splashed and flung clumps of muck and ooze in all directions.

When it finally came to rest, Ty was still hanging on, holding his breath and shaking with fear.

"Are you all right?" Normack called anxiously.

"Yeah, I'm okay," Ty said softly as he gave him a thumbs-up.

Then he took a deep breath and slowly started to pull himself loose. His leg was wedged in pretty deep, but as Ty started to pull himself free, he could feel something moving around his ankle. As soon as his foot was loose, he looked down and saw giant bugs with hooklike pincers and scorpion-like tails come pouring out from the hole. They started crawling on his shoes and up his legs. Ty tried desperately to knock them off as they began to swarm all over him. The more he struggled to knock them off, the more that log started to bounce and splash. Ty knew that if he lost his balance again, he would be going for a swim. He had to get off this floating pile of leaves fast, or he was going to be bug food. Frantically, Ty pulled out his spear and started to run.

Huge pieces of bark and branches were snapping off and flying in the air with every step he took. It was falling apart fast, and Ty was still pretty far from shore. It was all or nothing, so he started to run even faster. Suddenly, with a loud crack, the end of the tree snapped off and started to float away. With all the strength he had left, Ty dove for shore. A loud thud echoed across the swamp as Ty landed safely ashore!

"Nice moves," said Normack as he watched him crawl away from the shore and plop down on the gravel. "Nice moves, indeed!"

Normack came slowly slithering across what was left of that tree and made his way over to where Ty was sitting. As he looked down, he started to snicker. "With a jump like that, you must be a part frog too."

"Are you kidding me? I could jump twice that far to avoid landing in that stuff. If you think you're so good, then I'll race you up the hill to the Crystal Mountain."

"Wait, stop right there. You can't go that way!" Normack demanded. "You're headed straight for the land of the rock monster,

Grog. If that thing finds us, it'll grind us into dust. It can't stand anything trespassing on its land. Even the birds aren't safe when they fly over that place."

After Ty's little adventure crossing that swamp, he didn't want to listen to anything Normack had to say. "Don't be such a sissy, Normack. This is the quickest way to the Crystal Mountain, and I'm not afraid of anything!"

"Ty, you have no idea what you are getting yourself into! There's nothing sissy about avoiding a place that will put your life at risk! In fact, knowing when to enter a dangerous area and when to avoid one is a sign of maturity. That is a lesson that you need to learn fast before your pride gets us both killed!"

"Whatever," said Ty. "I'm not going to let anything stop me from saving my grandma, but if it will make you feel better, we can sneak past those hills, staying in the shadows and keeping quiet. You're scary, scary little monster poo, Groggy, will never know we were ever there. So pull up your big boy scales and let's get moving. It is a long way to that mountain, and I want to get as far away from this stinking pit as fast as I can!"

CHAPTER 3

The Mountain Is Alive

Silently, they started on their way up the steep hill full of thorn bushes and thick brush. Normack was a natural at stealth, and Ty traveled as quietly as a whisper. All you could hear was the sound of a cold breeze blowing down the valley and through the trees. Continuing on their journey, Ty and Normack quickly arrived at the top and slowly worked their way around to the edge of a sharp pile of boulders that was protruding up between two large evergreen trees.

Normack noticed something glittering up ahead. "What is that?"

"I'm not sure yet, but I think I might know what it is. When we get to the top of the next hill, we should be able to get a better look."

As they crept through the next valley, both Ty and Normack kept a sharp lookout for any sign of trouble. But when they got closer to the top of the next hill, Ty told Normack to wait behind a large grove of mulberry bushes, then crawled on his belly and peeked over the top of the hill. After a quick look, he crawled back to where Normack was and sat down with a disgusted look on his face.

"I was afraid of that. I was hoping I was wrong, but I know exactly what it is. Those are razor bushes up ahead, and they're deadlier than anything you can imagine. We have those bushes surrounding my village, and nothing can get through it without being sliced to ribbons. We have to find another way around."

"You make me laugh! You're so eager to run through Grog's home turf, but you tremble at the sight of some weeds."

"I told you before, I'm not afraid of you or anything else in the forest. But there's no way we'll ever make it across that."

"Take it easy, fish feet. I can help you get across, but you must trust me."

"All right, but we have to move quickly. I don't want to be caught out in the open. Those bushes are a long way away, and there's nothing to hide behind. We have to cross a pretty big field before we get there. When you're ready, we'll make a break for it. Ready, set, go!"

In a flash, those two took off racing across the field. Ty tried as hard as he could to keep up, but Normack was pulling ahead. The field that they were so desperately racing through was littered with large boulders and crushed tree trunks with splintered tops. Ty tried as hard as he could to jump over the smaller boulders and dodge the stumps as they raced to get out of the open. Normack looked over with a grin on his face, watching as Ty struggled to keep up as he slithered effortlessly back and forth and around every obstacle. It seemed to take forever to cross that pasture, but they made it safely to the edge of the razor bushes in less than a minute.

"What are we going to do now, Normack?"

"Just climb up on my back and hold on tight. I will carry you over these weeds, but you must never speak of this to anyone, ever. If anyone found out that you rode me like a horse, I will never live it down."

"Thank you. Thank you very much. I won't forget it, and I swear I'll never tell anyone. Now let's get this over with."

Ty didn't wait another second. He leaped up on Normack's hard and scaly back, then grabbed ahold of one of his scales as tight as he could. Normack slowly turned and glanced back at Ty to make sure he was ready, then with one smooth slithery motion, they gently rose and started to glide over those dangerous bushes. You could hear the sharp leaves scratching and slicing against Normack's thick scales as they brushed against that thick row of bushes just inches below Ty's legs.

As soon as they made it safely to the other side, Ty slid off and started jumping around. "Wow, that was so cool! Just like a roller-coaster ride in a carnival. I've got to try that again! But next time, I want some cotton candy."

"Very funny, fish feet, but you must keep quiet. We are not out of danger yet. Grog's territory goes all the way to the edge of the blue fields, and that's still far away. That thing could be anywhere."

Ty's little moment of fun was over; his smile and laughter faded away. He realized that they weren't even close to getting out of Grog's home turf, and the Crystal Mountain was still so far away. Ty nodded his head silently, and they continued their journey through the forest, not saying a word to each other until they made it out of that patch of woods and were standing next to another pasture pounded flat with shattered rocks and boulders. There were no more shadows to sneak around in, or any trees left to hide behind. They could see the blue fields just a couple hundred yards away, and Ty wasn't going to let anything stop him now.

"Hey, Normack, the coast looks clear. Let's go for it. All we've got to do is head straight over the next hill and we're home free."

"Don't be so sure, little one. We're not home free yet. It's still a long way to the blue fields."

"I know that," Ty whispered. "But I don't want to hang around here any longer than I have to, so come on."

They both took a deep breath to regain their confidence and headed across the open field. After climbing over a large, smooth boulder in the middle of the field, Ty stopped right in his tracks and gazed up ahead.

"Look, there it is. There's the Crystal Mountain just over the next hill. It's more beautiful than anything I've ever seen!" Ty was jumping up and down, bursting with excitement. "Check it out, Normack. When the sun hits it, it looks like a rainbow glowing on the ground. It must be one gigantic cluster of crystals."

"Would you be quiet?" hissed Normack. "If you ever want to see it up close, you have to stay quiet!"

"Okay, okay. I didn't mean to yell like that. You're right, let's get going."

Just as they started to climb down that boulder, the ground started to shake and rumble.

"Watch out, Normack! It's an earthquake!"

"I don't think it's an earthquake. I think we're in big trouble!"

Ty tried his best to keep his balance as the boulders rocked and rumbled under his feet. The hill was trembling so hard they had to dive for safety to the grass below.

"You've got to be kidding me!" Ty shouted as he watched the hill starting to move and sway. "This is not good! Let me guess, Normack. That's Grog."

"You're pretty smart. What gave it away?"

They frantically looked around for somewhere to run, but they were trapped. Slowly rising up from the deep pile of rubble was a creature made of solid rock. Its legs were wide and strong, and its body looked like someone had chiseled massive muscles on the side of a mountain. Ty looked over at Normack in shock; he couldn't believe how huge it was. Even though Ty was standing on the lip of a huge chunk of marble, he barely stood as tall as its waist. As it stretched its gigantic arms in the air, its muscles started to ripple in the bright sunlight. Ty started to panic.

"Pssst, Normack, what should we do?"

"Shhhh. Whatever you do, just don't make it mad!"

It seemed like an eternity went by as they stood there face-to-face with the rock monster. A shiver ran through Ty's soul as the sound of its powerful stone muscles grinding together when it turned its head and looked down on our two friends with its two bloodred eyes.

For a moment, Ty was frozen with fear, but he was able to gather a small bit of courage as he looked in its eyes. "Hey, Grog, I really hope you don't mind us cutting through your yard. We're just passing by on our way to that field over there. So you can just lie back down and go back to sleep. I swear we won't bother you at all."

Grog stared down at Ty and Normack and started to tremble. Then as Ty slowly started to step back away from that scary mountain of stone, it arched its back and raised its enormous fists in the air. Suddenly, it let out a mighty roar and slammed its fists into the ground. A thunderous blast rumbled across the land as a cloud of dust rose up and swirled around their legs.

"Guess not," muttered Ty as he took a big gulp and looked back at Normack.

"Run, Ty! Run for your life! I'll try to hold it down so you can escape! Now move quickly."

Normack struck as fast as lightning, wrapping all around Grog and started to squeeze it with all his might. "Run! Run now and you will be able to get away!"

"I won't leave you!" screamed Ty as he drew his bow and fired an arrow right into Grog's neck!

The arrow hit its mark with a mighty crack and shattered into a hundred pieces. Grog grabbed Normack behind his head and started to pound him ferociously.

"Run, Ty! Please! I can't hold him much longer!" begged Normack. "Get out of here now."

Boom! Boom! Boom! Grog's brutal punches sent shock waves rippling through Normack as he desperately tried to wrap around Grog and pin its arm down. Blow after blow, Ty watched helplessly as Normack slowly started to slide off Grog as his grip slowly faded away. Grog's vicious attack was taking its toll. Normack was being beaten badly.

Ty desperately wanted to do something, but he knew his weapons were useless. Grog continued to pound and pound on Normack as Ty frantically looked around for something, anything he could use to get that rock monster off his friend.

"What are you waiting for? Save yourself! Run to the blue fields! I can't hold him anymore. Just go!"

Ty turned and screamed, "That's it! I've got it." He quickly readied another arrow, drew back on his bow, and shot another arrow right in Grog's face! It shook its head wildly as the splinters from that arrow flew into its eyes. Grog let out a cold and hateful roar, then turned and looked right at Ty.

"What's the matter? Didn't you like that arrow? Well, maybe you will like this one better." boasted Ty as he drew back his bow once more and sent another arrow right between Grog's eyes.

As the splintered pieces of his arrow fell to the ground, Ty jumped up on a large boulder and screamed out as loud as he could, "You better put my friend down, or I am going to cut you up into bricks and build an outhouse out of you!"

Grog roared out with anger again. You could feel the electricity filling the air as Grog's heart filled with rage. With one powerful move, Grog ripped Normack off and threw him across the clearing right into a tree.

Smash! Crack! The tremendous blast rang out as huge chunks of that tree trunk shot off in every direction. Normack's head hit the ground with a hollow thud. His body twitched twice, then lay there motionless. Blood oozed from his mouth as his eyes slowly closed.

"You're going to pay for that, boulder butt!" Ty screamed, and he fired another arrow right into Grog's chest. "Now come and get me, you jerk!"

Ty started running as fast as he could back into the forest, but Grog was right behind him step for step. Who knew this pile of rocks could move so fast? The ground started to crack apart with every pounding step that Grog took. As Ty approached the forest, he really poured it on, weaving through the trees and leaping over the bushes as smoothly as a six-legged fire rasp. In fact, Ty was going so fast his legs were a blur, but Grog just kept on coming, smashing into dust every tree that stood in its way. Soon, Ty made it to the top of the ridge, and he could start to smell that awful stench again.

Ty ripped right down that hill, heading straight for the row of razor bushes. But that beast wasn't slowing down at all; it was right behind him. In fact, Grog was so close that if Ty slowed down or tried to turn around, he would be a goner. Ty thought he could outrun it, but it was too fast. He was too scared to stop, and there was nowhere else to go but straight into that razor-sharp death trap. Closer and closer, Ty came but he just kept running as fast as he could. When he was only inches away, Ty stuck his spear deep into the ground and flew over those bushes with one mighty leap!

Safely on the other side, Ty spun around and screamed, "Next time, you better get those rocks out of your pockets if you are going to catch me!"

Only Grog didn't stop. In fact, it didn't slow down at all. Ty dove behind a tree just seconds before Grog went crashing into the razor bushes. Ty watched in shock as the razor bushes shattered like a wall of glass, sending sharp and jagged pieces flying in every direction, ripping apart everything it touched. Ty peeked around that tree again and saw Grog just standing there without a scratch.

"I guess being made of stone has its privileges," muttered Ty. "But it looks like you just can't take a hint, boulder boy. So if you want a piece of me, just come and get it."

Ty bolted over the last hill, heading straight for the slimy, gross swamp.

Grog pounded his fists furiously against his chest as it watched Ty bolting through the woods. Then with one swipe of its huge hands, it ripped an old tree out of the ground and whipped it right at Ty's head. Ty dove to the ground just as it came screaming past his head like a cannonball.

Grog growled in anger and smashed the ground as the trunk went bouncing past Ty.

"You asked for it," shouted Ty as he jumped over the last hilltop, disappearing past the mulberry bushes.

Ty ran across the shore and jumped onto the tree bridge as fast as he could. Jumping from piece to piece, Ty made his way back across the busted-up bridge. As soon as he made it about halfway, Ty ducked down as low as he could behind an old crooked branch covered with moss and held on as tightly as he could, hoping that Grog wouldn't be able to see him.

A few moments later, Ty watched as Grog busted down the last few trees that stood in its way and came storming over the hill. Ty did everything he could to keep that log from rolling over as waves of muck and slime started to rock that tree bridge from the shock waves of Grog's thunderous steps.

With that busted old willow tree splashing back and forth, it only took a few seconds for Grog to spot Ty hanging on to that log for his dear life. Ty was now totally trapped, and with the tree bridge rolling wildly in that bubbling goop, he couldn't do a thing to get away.

Grog let out a loud and vicious growl and came running across the shore and onto the bridge after Ty. But as Grog closed in on Ty, the tree bridge started to crack and pop under its tremendous weight.

Without warning, the tree bridge snapped like a twig, sending them both flying into that murky swamp. Grog was splashing wildly in that murky mess, flinging clumps of mud and grime in every direction. In spite of everything it tried, there was no stopping it now. Grog was sinking fast, and in just moments, it was gone.

Ty struggled desperately to grab ahold of a piece of that tree so he could keep his head up out of the water, but with all of Grog's splashing, there was nothing left to grab on to; everything had floated away. That water was thick with muck and slime, making it impossible for Ty to pull himself free. The more Ty struggled, the harder it was for him to move. Ty was getting weaker, and the slime started to pull him down.

Slowly and quietly, the rushing waves of that black swamp grew still. The waters were quiet once more. There was only the soft sound of gently rustling leaves coming from the woods. There was no sign of Ty anywhere. He was gone too.

Suddenly, a huge figure came bursting out from the bushes along the shore. It was Normack!

"What happened here? Ty, where are you? Ty! Ty!"

Normack looked all around the shore, and the only footprints he could see led straight into the swamp. Normack slithered back and forth, flicking his tongue at every turn, trying to see any sign of where Ty could be. Just then, Normack spotted Ty's motionless body floating up slowly from the bottom of that gloomy swamp, covered with black ooze. His green eyes grew huge as he witnessed that awful sight. Without hesitating for a second, Normack dove in after him. Swishing back and forth as fast as any vipercon has ever done before, he swam over, snatched him up, and got him to shore.

"Wake up, fish feet! I won't let you die after what you've done for me, so you better wake up right now!"

Ty's body lay there motionless on the cold, hard, rocky ground. Normack yelled as loud as he could to wake him up, but it just didn't work. He knew that Ty must have swallowed some of that black swamp water. So he coiled around Ty and gave him a squeeze to push it out. A chunk of sludge shot out and splattered against Normack's chin as he clinched again and squeezed a little harder. Three more times he squeezed again and again before Ty slowly started to open his eyes and begin coughing up more of that stinking black ooze.

Normack bent down and shook his head. "You better learn to swim if you're going to try a stunt like that again. We better get out of here before Grog returns."

"We won't have to worry about boulder butt anymore," Ty mumbled as he coughed and gagged up that slimy mess.

"Why? What did you do?"

Ty sat up, pointing out toward the middle of the swamp. "Grog is somewhere out there, lying on the bottom! Considering that Grog's a rotten old rock monster, being trapped underwater shouldn't harm him at all. But that thing sure is in for a long walk if it ever wants to get out of that stink hole. Enough talk about pebble brains. I think I am going to get sick, and I need a bath, and I mean right now."

So Ty staggered to his feet, headed for the first clean puddle he saw and dove right in.

"What are you doing? At least you don't smell like rotten fish feet anymore. I think it is an improvement!" Normack chuckled while he watched Ty splashing around.

CHAPTER 4

An Unexpected Surprise

The way back to the great Crystal Mountain went by like a flash, especially since Grog had trampled down every tree and razor bush that stood in his way (and believe me, that made a very nice road back). In no time at all, they were strolling through the blue meadows headed to the base of that magnificent mountain. It looked even more beautiful up close, shining and glistening in the afternoon sun.

However, Normack started to complain that he was feeling very tired and quite sore. That fight he had with Grog must have worn him out.

"I just need to rest for a little while," hissed Normack. "I see a nice comfortable place in a clearing next to that tall silver tree, and it's got my name all over it. So I'll see you in a little bit."

Ty just smiled. "Go ahead and relax for a while and get some rest. You've earned it. I'm going to take a look around. I'll be back in about an hour to check up on you, but if you need me, I'm going to explore those caves next to that tall pillar over there."

Normack just peeked over to where Ty was pointing and let out a sigh. "No problem, fish feet. I will see you in a while."

Ty just shook his head and smiled as he walked by Normack. But when he started to walk around him, he stepped in some sticky slime oozing out from under one of his scales.

"Yuck! What in the world is that? Hey, Normack, what's up with your scale over here? Is that normal?"

"My scales, what are you talking about? I'm fine. Just go ahead and check out that cave. I'll catch up with you later," snapped Normack as nestled his head down in the soft grass.

"I'm talking about this goop all over your side," Ty replied as he pointed at a puddle of nasty yellowy slime oozing out from under one of Normack's scales.

"I don't know what you're talking about. The only thing wrong with me is that, thanks to Grog, I have a pounding headache and my side feels a bit sore from getting smashed against a tree."

"Hey, I'm not kidding here. I think you got an infection. My mom always said if you have a cut and don't keep it clean, it'll get infected. So if you have a cut under your scale, that little swim you had in that swamp could cause a really bad infection. This looks serious, Normack. This goop dripping out over here stinks worse than that swamp. Let me just check this out for you because there's something's not right."

"Whatever. Just hurry up. I don't need anybody poking around me while I try to get some rest!"

"Now this shouldn't hurt a bit. All I have to do is to pry up on this scale a little to get a better look."

Ty reached down and tried to pull back on Normack's scale, but he couldn't get his fingers underneath it far enough to pull it back. He stepped back and looked around for something he could use to help him get a better look at Normack's side. Then he saw the perfect thing. He walked back and grabbed his spear and used it to gently pry his scale up a little bit.

"That's perfect," Ty said. "Just stay still for a minute while I take a look."

When he knelt on the ground and looked underneath that scale, Ty froze in fear. "Holy thunder!" screamed Ty! "It's a life leech. You have a life leech stuck on you, Normack. That's why you're so tired and can't move. We have to get that thing off right now!"

"What in the world are you talking about?" muttered Normack.

"I said it's a life leech, you big dumb snake. They live on the flesh and life force of anything they can sink their teeth into, and the only thing that's left after a life leech is done feeding is a dried-up, hollow body!"

Normack looked over to where Ty was kneeling. "You're crazy! No leech could ever bite through my scales no matter how tough they are."

"I never said it bit through your scales. It must have squirmed between them when you dove into the black swamp to save my life."

"Ty, that sounds ridiculous. Look around you. Leeches crawl around on the ground, and I've never been attacked by one of your life leeches before!"

"Normack, I'm not kidding! Just listen. My Dad taught me all about these things. Life leeches can only survive in really dark places like that swamp because if they get caught in the sunlight for very long, their bodies dry out and get so hard it's like they turn to steel. That's why you've never see one on the ground before. They can't survive in the woods."

"Well then, if you know so much about life leeches, what are you waiting for? Pull it off and step on it!"

"Normack, you don't understand! My dad said that they can move as fast as lightning, and the only way you can kill one is to capture it in a net and leave it in the sun. But we don't have a net, and we don't have enough time to make one. I don't know what to do, Normack! I just don't know what to do!"

Ty really started to panic; he ran all around, trying to think of some way he could get that monster off Normack and trap it before it killed him.

"I've got to find something to use and fast, Normack! Don't worry! I'll figure something out," shouted Ty in desperation.

He ran to the Crystal Mountain, hoping to find something he could use to defeat a life leech. There was absolutely nothing around, and Ty looked everywhere. Then as fast as he could, Ty ran back to Normack and told him, "I just won't give up on you. There's always something you can do."

Ty was getting very nervous because Normack was getting weaker and weaker; he barely had enough strength left to keep his eyes open. Normack was running out of time. Ty ran back to the mountainside and started digging around the crystals again. He knew if he had a rope, he could tie it around that thing and rip it off. But there was nothing around he could use. Ty turned around and, in pure frustration, punched that crystal wall as hard as he could. *Crack!* The sound echoed across the ground. Ty grabbed his fist and screamed out in pain because it felt like he nearly broke every bone in his hand on that stupid rock. After stomping around, trying to get over the pain, he looked back at that spot where he smacked that rock and was nearly blinded by the light shining off it.

"That's it! I've got it!" Ty screamed. "This can work. Normack, I've got an idea. I just hope that I have enough time."

Moving as fast as he could, Ty ripped off his jacket and started rubbing and cleaning off all the dirt and grime from that crystal. He rubbed that thing so hard it sparkled like a mirror!

"Over here, Normack," yelled Ty. "You've got to come over here, right here. It's the only way to get that thing off you."

Normack struggled to open his eyes and looked over at Ty. "I don't think I can make it. I don't have enough strength left."

"You got to!" Ty screamed. "It's your only chance. Now get your scaly butt over here!"

Normack gathered all his strength and slowly moved toward Ty.

"That's it, just a little further."

With the very last bit of energy that Normack could muster, he made it to the spot that Ty was pointing to, then collapsed, exhausted. There was no more time left. This had to work, and it had to work right now! Ty grabbed his spear, wedged it deep under Normack's scale, and started prying it back as hard as he could. He pulled back that scale so far that he could see that huge leech feasting on what life Normack had left. It was time to get rid of this monster!

Ty knew that if he tried to stab it with his spear, he might miss and hurt Normack. So he held his spear like a baseball bat and swung it with all his might and smacked that life leech right on its back. *Crack!* He smacked that slimeball so hard his spear snapped in half. If that didn't get its attention, nothing would.

The moment Ty's spear snapped in half, that horrible creature let out a monstrous squeal that sounded like a vampire bat ripping into its prey. In a flash, it jerked its head out from under Normack's scale, and its three bright yellow eyes turned jet-black as it stared deep into Ty's eyes.

Ty jumped back as it let out another bone-chilling screech and opened up its blood-filled mouth. All he could see was row after row of razor-sharp green teeth, spinning around and around, still dripping with Normack's blood. Ty was never more scared in his life. He closed his eyes for a second and wished that his dad was there with him, but he was all alone, staring right down the throat of that beast.

Ty stood his ground and looked that thing right in its eyes. Then he opened his arms out wide, showing that beast his bare chest and screamed as loud as he could, "If you want a piece of me, just come and get it!"

With a high-pitched shriek, it coiled up and prepared to attack. Quick as lightning, that life leech bolted out from under Normack's scale, heading straight for Ty's chest so fast he didn't have time to move!

Whack! It hit hard. The sickening sound of crushing flesh rippled across the meadow.

"Oh, man… it worked! I knocked it out cold. That thing thought it was going to feast on me, but it was just my reflection on that crystal. When that slug tried to sink its teeth into my chest, all he got was a mouthful of rock! Did you hear me, Normack? I made that thing bite stone! That disgusting monster won't be feasting on anything anymore. I think it knocked all its teeth out too. You have to get up now. We got to get out of here fast. I don't want to be around when that thing wakes up."

Normack just opened his eyes for a moment. "You go, Ty. I'm just going to stay here and rest for a while. Don't worry about me. That thing's way too big now to fit under my scales. I'll be just fine."

"All right," Ty said. "But if you don't mind, I want to check out where that thing had ahold of you first."

Ty crept as carefully as he could around that life leech so he wouldn't wake it up, grabbed what was left of his spear, pried up that scale once again, and took a peek.

"Well, bud, it looks like you lost a lot of blood. The good news is the wound doesn't look too deep and the bleeding has stopped. It's a good thing my mom is a doctor. I know exactly what to do. There are plenty of healing plants growing all around these woods. I'll have you all fixed up in no time."

Ty pulled up a handful of sponge moss that was growing behind the silver tree and used it as a Band-Aid. But when Ty stepped over that life leech on his way to the forest, he noticed a pool of green blood by its head.

"Hey, wait a minute, that life leech isn't knocked out. It's dead! Hey, Normack, it's dead. It's really dead!" screamed Ty as he started jumping up and down.

Normack smiled and nodded his head. "I have to admit, you sure are resourceful. It must have died instantly when it slammed into that crystal wall. We won't have to worry about that beast anymore."

But while Ty stood gloating over that dead life leech, he looked around and suddenly realized that he was almost out of weapons. His spear was broken; there were only two arrows left. His knife was dull and chipped badly from slamming it into that tree. Ty looked over at the forest's edge, then started to get that feeling that he would never get out of there alive if he didn't do something about it. The weapons he had weren't going to be good enough. He desperately needed better and stronger weapons than the ones he had now. Ty knew he could easily repair his broken spear with a new staff, except it still wouldn't be strong enough if he ran across any really tough creatures like that rinog.

Once again, Ty started searching for something he could use to make some weapons that would be strong enough to take him through his quest. Now those crystals were very strong, but they just weren't sharp enough to use. That's when Ty looked down at that disgusting life leech lying dead in the sun and knew just what he had to do. Instead of letting that life leech go to waste, he would use its hide to make everything he needed. Since Ty had ruined his jacket cleaning off that crystal, he made himself a vest, then laid it out on top of the brightest crystal he could find in order for it to cure hard and strong. Next, he took a big piece, stretched it over a smooth curved boulder, and formed it into a perfect shield. Ty started to grin as he smoothed it out and trimmed off its ragged edges. He knew right away that if he was able to get it to cure properly, it would stand up to anything that place could ever dish out.

The one thing he needed more than anything else was an invincible weapon. So Ty took his time and polished a golden crystal as smooth and bright as he could, then laid a piece as long as his arm gently on top of it. He took great care in shaping it into the perfect sword, then used the fang he took from Normack to form a mighty hilt. He knew right away that a sword created from the hide of a life leech would be the strongest weapon ever created.

When he was done, Ty placed another golden crystal on top to keep it perfectly flat and in perfect shape while it dried. However, when Ty placed those two crystals together, a blinding golden light shot out from between them like a starburst, knocking him to the ground. He knew right away that sword he made would be incredibly special.

Finally, as he was starting to run out of time, he took what was left and cut it into one long strip and stretched it out as tight as he could between two trees. Then he ran around, flipping over every flat rock he could see, hoping to find some oily stipple moss. After searching under every rock in the area, he was about to give up until he flipped over a long crystal shard at the edge of the forest and found a nice thick batch of that oily, sludgy mess.

"This might work," he said softly to himself because he knew that if there was anything that could stop a life leech skin from turning hard, it had been that slimy sludge. So he scooped up a nice, big, dripping handful, ran back, and smeared it all over that strip so it would slowly soak in and keep it from drying out.

"What were you doing over there?" whispered Normack as Ty walked back to see how he was doing.

"Well, I was trying to make a rope. But if that stipple moss doesn't work, I guess I just made one really long and slippery pole." Ty chuckled as he wiped his hands off in the dirt.

For once, Ty figured he had everything he needed to survive this terrible place, or at least he would finally have a fighting chance.

Ty turned and looked at Normack and said, "What you need now is some food to help you build up your strength and some medicine to help your injuries heal. Since my sword is drying, I'll just take my bow and go hunting to get you something to eat. Now you save your strength and warm yourself in the sun, and I'll be back soon."

Normack nodded his head and closed his eyes. He knew that he could trust his friend. Normack had never put that much trust in anyone else, but after what just happened, he knew that he could trust Ty with his life.

CHAPTER 5

Alone Again In The
Shadow Forest

Ty smiled, grabbed his knife and bow, and then headed for the forest. He wasn't sure what he could get for Normack to eat, but the forest was big and he wouldn't go back without something. Unfortunately, Ty knew that this could turn out to be a bigger challenge than he would admit. The only hunting he had ever done was for frogs and turtles, back by the river at home. So having a fifty-foot vipercon to feed was going to be a challenge.

As he made his way across the blue meadow, he started to think about all the adventures he had been through. Ty would never have imagined his trip into the Shadow Forest would've turned out like it had. Before long, Ty was back in the shade of that creepy forest again, except this time, instead of running from the beasts that live in the forest, he was looking to take one down.

He walked through the trees, moving as silently as a ghost. His senses felt sharp and crisp; he could smell the freshly fallen leaves, and the sound of the trees swaying in the slight breeze was like the soft music that fills the air in a dream.

There were animal tracks all around him. Some he could recognize, like those of a small rabbit and a deer, but the tracks he found next to a boulder made him quite nervous. Those tracks definitely belonged to a huge wolf. The wolf tracks, thank goodness, seemed to be a couple days old, but the deer tracks were fresh.

Finally, some good luck for a change, Ty thought to himself. *Bringing back a deer for Normack would get his strength back quickly. But if I run into a wolf out here, I'm going to be in big trouble.*

Ty picked up a few leaves, then slowly let them float out of his hands, watching as they drifted to the ground, thinking, *Perfect, the wind is blowing towards me and that means nothing out here in this creepy place will get a whiff of my scent until it's too late.* Ty started to follow those deer tracks through the forest, staying in the shadows and moving as quietly as he could. They led Ty through fields of thick brush and over steep hills and, finally, brought him into a small valley full of rich berry bushes and lush green trees.

His eyes filled with excitement, Ty knew that deer was close. Staying hidden behind a tree, he studied the area ahead, paying close attention to every place a deer could be hiding behind. He was hoping to spot any sign that it went through the field like bent twigs, folded-over grass, or maybe even a bird suddenly springing up and flying away. The more he watched, the more disappointed he got. Even the tracks he was following seemed to disappear into the soft grass ahead.

Just another dead end, Ty thought, but just as he was going to give up, he heard some leaves rustling up ahead. The hairs on the back of his neck started to tingle. That wasn't the sound of leaves rustling in the wind. There was something else there, something big. Up ahead, on the far side of the clearing, he watched as some bushes moved just a little bit. With a grin on his face, Ty got down on his belly and crawled closer to that berry bush. Suddenly, the sound of a small twig snapping rang out beneath him. He froze for a second, then rolled behind a large tree, and held his breath. He peeked around the tree and saw the bushes rustle again; there was definitely something in there.

Ty sat there quietly, watching and squinting his eyes as hard as he could to make out what was lurking behind those leaves. That's when he started to piece together the different pattern of tracks he was following: the deer tracks heading off into the woods alone and the wolf tracks crossing the deer's path in a zigzag pattern. Ty wasn't the only thing hunting that deer. That wolf must be around here somewhere, and if it couldn't have that deer, then it just might try to hunt him instead.

He watched silently as the bushes slowly swayed to the side as something large started pushing against it. You could hear the faint sound of cautious footsteps walking across the soft leaves, like a predator on the prowl. Whatever was behind that brush was starting to come out. Ty reached for his bow, slid an arrow between his fingers, and held his breath as a large shadow drifted between the twigs, headed for the clearing.

There it was, the biggest deer he had ever seen. What a perfect shot. It had no idea that Ty was there as it bowed its head to nibble the grass. Suddenly, the deer twitched and stood up straight. You could see its huge muscles rippling as it nervously looked around. Ty held his breath and stayed perfectly still, hoping the deer wouldn't see him. It seemed like time slowed down and every second crawled by as that deer scanned the forest for danger.

What a magnificent animal, Ty thought. It looked so strong and fearless standing there with the sun glistening off its antlers. Ty knew what he had to do and slowly drew back his bowstring, holding his breath to steady his aim. He gazed deeply into those dark brown eyes as he drifted his aim to its heart.

"I just can't do it," Ty whispered in frustration.

He closed his eyes and slowly exhaled. A sense of calm ran through his body like a warm wave as he lowered his bow and slung it back over his shoulder. He watched in amazement as it flinched once more and started to graze again. Ty thought about Normack and the promise he had made. But it he just couldn't bring himself to do it. So Ty slowly took a step out from behind that tree to see that remarkable animal better. In an instant, the deer's head snapped back, quickly spotting Ty standing there. Hesitating just for a moment, as if to say thank you, it raised its front hoofs up and bolted for the safety of the forest. Ty stood there just watching as the bushes swayed back and forth as it disappeared into the shadows.

Ty started to head back to the crystal mountain, upset with himself that he didn't kill the deer, but deep down inside, he knew that he had done the right thing. He figured that it wasn't a total loss because he remembered that, while he was tracking the deer, he had passed some aloe plants that he could use for Normack's wounds and a strong willow tree with some real old bark that he could use to make some medicine to ease his friend's pain.

The aloe plants were going to be easy to get. They were growing right next to the trail he was following; so on his way back, he just broke off a handful of leaves and filled his pockets up.

The next thing on his list was the willow bark, which was going to be a bit harder to get because it was growing on the other side of a creek. It might not seem like such a big deal, but the sides of the creek were really steep and muddy. Ty knew that if he wasn't careful, he could fall into the fast-moving water below and drown. So he took his time, walked downstream a bit, and found a safer place to cross. In no time at all, he was standing on the other side and making his way back to the willow tree.

Considering how big Normack was, Ty knew he needed the strongest medicine bark he could get his hands on. That meant he needed to get some off the very top branches. So when Ty got back to that great willow tree, he stood there for a minute, looking it over very carefully, and then with a big, excited grin, he grabbed the closest branch and swung into action. He pounced effortlessly from limb to limb, getting higher and higher. Ty was having fun again as he raced to the very top of that tree, but his fun seemed to end in a flash as he flipped over the last twisted limb and reached the top of that huge tree. He sat down on that last crooked limb, pulled out his knife, and went to work, stripping huge handfuls of fresh bark from the most powerful parts of the tree. Within minutes, he had everything he needed and stuffed his pouch to the top.

While sitting high in the tree, Ty could see the top of the crystal mountain glittering in the sun. The magnificent colors streaming off it made his heart start pounding as the excitement rushed through his veins. *There had to be huge deposits of blue fire rubies scattered all over that mountain*, he thought. Overwhelmed with anticipation, he started swinging and jumping from branch to branch, making his way back down. When Ty made it to the bottom branch, he dove off it like a springboard and hit the ground so hard that his legs sank into the sand up to his knees. Ty took one look at his legs as he tried to wiggle out and then burst out laughing. "Now that's how you stick a landing!"

After Ty had a good laugh, he tried to get out, but he couldn't move an inch; he was really stuck. All he needed was some good leverage to get him out, and the only thing close enough for him to grab was one of the tree's thick roots.

That will work, Ty thought to himself as he leaned out for the root, but as he stretched across the ground, he heard a loud snap. *What in the world was that?* Ty wondered. Then another pop rang out and the ground started to shake. Ty looked around and held on tight. *This is definitely not going to be good.*

In a flash, the ground started to crumble and collapse. Ty kept struggling to drag himself free. Another chunk of dirt gave way and disappeared into a crack in the ground, and then, suddenly, another snap rang out and Ty sank up to his chest. He knew he had to get out of this mess fast, so he stretched out as far as he could and had just barely gotten a few fingers around that old tree root when the rest of the ground around him fell away. He hung on to that root with all his might as dirt and rocks disappeared into a deep crevice below.

After a few seconds had passed, the ground stopped shaking and Ty was still there, swinging back and forth from that old slippery root. Ty shook off a clump of mud stuck to his back and shouted down that deep, dark hole, "You have to do better than that to get me!" then reached up with his other hand, grabbed that old root as it snapped in half, sending him tumbling down the hole. Bouncing and crashed into the rocky walls of that cavern, he fell helplessly into the darkness. A hollow thud echoed through the cave when Ty slammed to the ground. He lay there motionless as dirt sprinkled down and covered the floor.

As he lay there helplessly, the cave seemed to come alive with all sorts of creepy bugs. Bats filled the air and centipedes roamed the ground. Huge, hairy spiders, the size of your fist, started coming out from the shadows in every direction. They scurried across the floor, then jumped all over Ty, spinning their webs as fast as they could. Soon, a silky blanket covered his arms and legs, pinning him to the ground. As the giant spiders crawled all over Ty, their hairy legs started to tickle and scratch. Ty woke up just as a spider started to cast its web across his face.

"What in the world is going on?" Ty yelled. "And what is this gunk?"

As Ty frantically looked around, one of those giant spiders walked across his chest and down his leg.

"Get off me, you eight-legged creep!" screamed Ty.

He tried to knock it off, but he couldn't even move. Even though he pulled with all his might to free himself, the spiderwebs were too strong. All he could manage to do was stretch them out just a few inches. He struggled as hard as he could and, finally, was able to get ahold of his knife.

"Now you're in big trouble," said Ty.

He worked fast, slashing and cutting his way through that web of death. When Ty finally freed himself, he jumped up and started kicking those spiders across the cavern and stomping the rest of them into the ground. For the next few minutes, Ty just stood there, peeling that sticky web off and flicking it to the ground.

Ty took a look around that damp and musty place and knew he could be stuck there for a very long time. The walls of that cavern were so loose and crumbly that every time he tried to climb up, big chunks of dirt and rocks peeled away and came crashing down. He had to find another way out. He looked around, saw a little flicker of light squeezing out from a crack in the cavern wall, and mumbled to himself, "Cool, there's some daylight up ahead. Getting out shouldn't be too hard."

Ty started to feel his way through that dark and creepy cavern. He was having a real hard time feeling his way through the darkness, tripping over the crooked roots and shattered rocks scattered across the ground. But at least it became easier the closer he got to that light. Just as Ty walked around the last corner and peered through that crack, he stopped right in his tracks.

Ty found himself standing in the opening of an even larger cave with large deposits of star crystals growing out of the walls. Ty had never seen so many star crystals in one place before in his whole life; the whole cave was shining as bright as day!

"All right!" Ty yelled out at the top of his voice. "Nothing can stop me now!"

Ty knew right then and there that his search for the blue fire rubies just got a whole lot easier. With a huge smile on his face, he climbed right up to the biggest one he could reach and ripped it out of the wall. The bright white light that shot out of that crystal nearly blinded him. Instantly, he knew that he would never again have a problem making his way through any of those deep, dark caves ever again. He quickly put that star crystal to good use and ran out of that cavern as fast as his legs could go. *This is so cool*, Ty thought. *I can't wait to show Normack what I had found.*

Ty easily followed the tunnels and walked boldly out of that cave with his head held high and with new confidence that nothing was going to stop him now. Just as he cleared the entrance of that cave, Ty saw something out of the corner of his eye, moving around behind the bushes right next to the cave, and he ducked down a little bit to get a better look.

"Wow, would you look at that," said Ty.

He crept slowly around the side of that bush, taking great care not to make a sound. When Ty was inches away, he silently pulled out his knife and dove right in. The bushes shook wildly as Ty fought. In just a few moments, those bushes stopped shaking and the sounds of a life and death struggle slowly faded away.

Ty stood up slowly, covered with scratches from wrestling inside that twisted thick bush. With a smile on his face, Ty pulled out his prize. It was a huge white chicken flapping its wings violently and making a big racket, but Ty wasn't going to let this one get away.

Well, it's not as big as a deer, Ty thought to himself. *But Mom always says there's nothing better than chicken soup to help you feel better.* So Ty proudly headed back to the crystal mountain with that chicken held tightly in his grip.

It felt like he was gone for hours, but when Ty finally made it back to the blue meadow, he could see Normack still asleep in the warm summer sun.

"Hey, Normack," yelled Ty with excitement. "I bought you something to eat and some medicine too."

As Ty headed across the meadow, he made a very big mistake, a mistake that could have cost him his life. For a moment, he forgot that he was still in the Shadow Forest and forgot that can kill you quick.

You see, Ty causally strolled across that field, not paying any attention to what was around him anymore. All he was thinking about was what he had to do in order to make the medicine for Normack and how proud he was for finding a star crystal and capturing lunch. When he got about halfway through the field, he heard something running through the tall grass behind him. Ty spun around quickly to see what it was, but he couldn't see a thing.

Ty knew deep in his bones that he was in big trouble, so he took off running as fast as he could. The sound of footsteps turned into a steady pounding, getting closer and closer. When he looked over his shoulder, the only thing he saw was the tall grass flying in the air, cutting a path, heading straight for him. Ty dropped that chicken and poured on all the speed he had left, but in a split second, it felt like someone clobbered him in the back with a sledgehammer, sending him tumbling across the ground.

That was when Ty finally saw what was after him. His eyes filled with shock and fear as he watched a five-foot-tall vicious cave rat creeping closer and closer. Its long, oily black hair and razor-sharp yellow teeth shined with the blood of its last victim. It must have followed him from those caverns because cave rats rarely ever come out in the daylight.

Ty lay on his back, kicking and struggling as hard as he could, trying to keep that rat away long enough so he could escape. With a loud smack, Ty kicked it hard in the head, sending it tumbling backward into the grass. When Ty spun around and started to get up, it pounced again, pinning him to the ground. Instantly, Ty reached up and grabbed that thing by its throat, trying desperately to stop it

DAVID WALKER

from sinking its teeth deep into his chest. Ty fought back with every ounce of energy he had as it snapped and chomped wildly just inches from Ty's face. While they were wrestling on the ground, Ty managed to snatch his knife from his side and jabbed it into its mouth, but the beast just bit down hard, snapping his stone knife in half with its sharp teeth.

With both hands, Ty grabbed its throat again as hard as he could and shoved it straight back. The rat flew back onto its hind legs, shook its head wildly, and pounced again.

This time, Ty wasn't so lucky. That beast landed right on Ty's chest and used its paws to pin both of Ty's hands right to the ground. Ty struggled with all his might to get up, but he couldn't move at all. He was trapped. Ty looked up into those beady red eyes and watched helplessly as it opened its mouth up wide. He could see bits of flesh that was still stuck in its teeth, and he could smell the nasty stench of rotting flesh oozing out from that rat. That's when he heard a sound that he would never forget—the crunch of teeth slicing through bone.

Ty was in shock, frozen solid on the ground. He couldn't believe his eyes as he watched Normack sink his fangs deep into that filthy rat's chest. Twisting and spinning savagely, Normack had it trapped in his coils in a blink of an eye.

Normack looked down at Ty with a smile and asked, "How did you know that there's nothing better than a cave rat to help you feel better? Next time, if I were you, I wouldn't get so close to them. They do have a nasty bite if you're not careful."

"Oh, that's disgusting," Ty said as he watched the rat's tail slide down Normack throat. "By the way, Normack, how did you do that with one fang missing?"

"What do you mean? I have all four of my fangs. Sometimes a vipercon can lose a fang when we strike or when a small meal rips one out! So they grow back quickly" explained Normack.

Ty looked at Normack and laughed. "After you're done eating that rat, I want to put this medicine on you to help you heal. In the meantime, I guess I will have some chicken for lunch. That is if I can find it again."

48

"You're going to eat a bird? Now that's gross."

Ty just laughed a little and shook his head. He knew that Normack just saved his life, and he was still shaking a bit. "If you don't mind, I'll meet you back at the mountain. I've got a chicken to catch. Again!"

CHAPTER 6

The Search Continues

On their walk back to the crystal mountain, Ty picked up some dry twigs and sticks to make a fire so he could cook his lunch. He made a grand fire next to the crystal pillars and surrounded it with pieces of shattered stones to keep it from getting out of control, just like his dad did when they went camping.

While Ty's food was cooking, he reached into his bag, pulled out the willow bark, and started to grind it into powder between two pieces of crystals. He picked out all the black flakes that would make the medicine bitter and gritty. When he had made a pile of soft white powder large enough to fill the palm of his hand, he smiled brightly because he knew he had made the medicine right, and it looked like it was going to be perfect to help Normack.

"Hey, Normack, this is aspirin. It's a powerful medicine that will ease your pain from that battle you had with Grog. I learned how to make it from watching my mom. All you have to do is swallow it and you'll start feeling a lot better real quick." Ty wrapped it up in some leaves so Normack didn't have to taste it and dropped it on Normack tongue.

"Thank you, Ty. I didn't know your mom was a witch."

"She's not a witch, she's a doctor. She helps the people at home when they get hurt or need medicine. Now I picked up some more stuff here that will help that wound under your scale heal quicker. So I have to take a look under that scale again."

"Whatever you say, little doctor," Normack hissed gently as he slithered over to Ty.

Normack laid his head down in the cool grass and tried very hard to relax his scales so they would be easier to pull back. When Ty pried up the scale that was still covered with a little bit of slime, he was amazed at how well it was healing.

"Normack, this doesn't look as bad as I thought it would. But I'll still spread some aloe on it to make sure that you won't get an infection."

He split the aloe leaf open, scraped out the gel, and put it under Normack's scale. Then he used a little that was left over to smear on his own scrapes that he got tumbling down that hole and fighting that cave rat.

"Normack, there's one more thing you could use, and I think it might be the most important thing I can do for you," said Ty in a kind of sarcastic voice, then walked over to the silver tree that Normack was lying under when they first got to the crystal mountain and picked a few leaves from a small plant that was growing between its roots.

"Now, Normack, you have to chew these up good and swish it around your mouth before you swallow it. Okay?"

Normack agreed and did just what he was told. "This taste pretty good," Normack admitted. "What is this medicine going to do?"

"That's the one thing you needed the most. They're called mint leaves, and they can wipe out the worst case of rat breath that you can come up with."

"What did you say?" shouted Normack. "You tricked me. Tell me, little man-child. If that works so well on my breath, then why don't you use a handful on those fish feet of yours?"

Ty started to laugh real hard and then grabbed a big handful of mint leaves. "I don't know about that, but let's find out, Normack." Ty started rubbing them all over his feet. Those two were laughing and having a great time picking on each other.

Ty's meal was finally done to a wonderful golden brown. He pulled it off the fire and offered some to Normack, but he just shook his head and told him that the rat meal he had was enough.

After a few minutes went by, Ty started to think about how close he had come to being eaten alive and the laughter stopped. Things didn't seem to be very funny anymore. When Ty finished his meal, he looked over at the armor that he had made and knew it was time to get serious and get what he came for. He kicked some sand on the fire and stirred the coals to make sure it was smothered out real good. Then he walked over, picked up the armor, and was shocked to find out that it was as light as a feather. Ty sure hoped that it was going to fit because it wouldn't bend or flex no matter how hard he tried. It took a while to squeeze into that armor, but it fit him better than he could have ever hoped for.

Next, he grabbed his shield, but it felt like it was made of cardboard. *Boy, this doesn't seem like it's going to be strong enough to stop an attack from a butterfly*, Ty thought. He knew he had better test it out before he had to use it in battle, so he looked around for something to test it on. Not far from the silver tree, he found a crystal as hard as a diamond growing out of the mountainside. This was going to be a perfect test. Ty reached back and smacked the shield on that crystal with all his might. Boom! That blast echoed across the field. Ty stood there with his mouth wide open; he couldn't believe his eyes. That crystal shattered into a million pieces.

"Hey, Normack, that crystal just shattered like glass, and I didn't even feel a thing." Ty took a real good look at that shield where he hit that crystal, and there wasn't a single scratch on it. That armor and shield turned out ten times stronger than what he was hoping for.

Ty clipped his shield on his side and headed over to where he had that leech skin smeared with moss hanging. He hoped that his trick worked and he could still use it for a rope. When he got there, he was totally surprised that it was still flexible and as strong as steel. Ty had done a great job making sure that it didn't cure too fast and keeping it from turning into a long steel pole. With a grin on his face, he quickly rolled up the rope and slung it over his shoulder.

With a deep breath, the time had finally come to claim his sword. Ty was kind of nervous as he made his way back to where it was hidden. As he walked around the back side of the mountain, he saw that the golden light was still sparking and shooting out from between those two crystals, except it was twice as intense as before. With each step he took, his heart started beating faster and faster as the soft humming sound of racing electricity started to emanate from between those crystals.

Ty stood in the glow of the light, nervous and excited. He slowly reached out and lightly felt the top crystal, then pulled his hand back quickly in surprise. The crystal was as cold as ice around the edges but hot as dragon's breath across the top. Ty took another deep breath, gathered his nerve, reached down, picked up a few thick leaves, and used them to protect his hands. Then with all his might, he lifted that heavy crystal from atop his sword and threw it to the ground. A burst of light shot out across the field like lightning and lit up the Shadow Forest for miles. That was when he first saw his mighty sword. It's black blade shimmered and sparkled with power in the golden light and its ivory white vipercon fang hilt was covered with a layer of icy frost. Ty stood there for a few minutes, watching as the beautiful light flickered like fire across the crystal, then he took another deep breath and reached out to pick it up. The moment he touched its hilt, the humming stopped and the golden light flickered and went out.

As he lifted his sword, small sparks shot out from the crystal and ran up his arm and through his body. It was as if the incredible power of the crystal mountain was unleashed into that sword.

Ty looked behind him at the crystal mountain, then across the field to the edge of the Shadow Forest. That uneasy feeling in the pit of his stomach went away in the blink of an eye. He no longer feared cave rats, huge wolves, or any other creature that roamed in the shadows. For the very first time since he came to that forest, he felt truly safe and in control of everything around him. In that moment, Ty stopped being a boy and saw the world through the eyes of a man.

Standing tall, with his sword held high, Ty shouted boldly into the sky, "I came here into these woods on a quest, and no creature great or small can stop me. So hear these words and be warned because if you try, you will be defeated!"

Just then, Normack came rushing around the corner, wondering what all the commotion was about. When he saw Ty standing there with his armor shining in the sun and his sword held high, his green eyes opened wide; he froze solid in disbelief.

"Is that you, Ty?" Normack asked, his voice full of wonderment.

Ty spun around and put his sword away. "Yes, of course, it's me. What in the world is wrong with you, Normack? It looks like you have seen a ghost or something!"

"I'm okay," stuttered Normack as he slid around Ty's side. "You just look so different, and the way you're standing there reminds me of a story about a mighty warrior."

Normack started to tell Ty the story about a mighty warrior that battled many creatures, and when he came out of the Shadow Forest, he flew across the sky like an eagle to battle against the mightiest creature of all.

Ty smiled and nodded his head. "I know all about that story too. My history teacher has told us all about it. Ms. Sue said that the warrior's name was Cobasfang."

Ty looked down at his armor and then at Normack and busted out laughing, saying, "You thought I was Cobasfang? That's the craziest thing I've ever heard. I'm only a boy, not to mention that I don't have any wings and I can't fly."

"I know you're not Cobasfang, but the way you were standing there with the light shining on that sword just made me think of the story, that's all. Anyway, there is no way a warrior as great as Cobasfang could ever walk around in these woods with feet that smell as bad as yours do."

Ty looked up at Normack and started laughing again.

"Well, Normack, I hope you're done making fun of my feet because I'm dying to get inside some of these caves and find some blue fire rubies."

"I'm not done making fun of you yet, little man-child. But if you're ready, I'll stop for a while and help you look in those caves too."

Ty had a little smirk on his face because he had a smart-aleck comment he was going to say, but he was so anxious to start looking he could hardly control himself. There were so many caves to explore; they didn't know where to start. So they decided to split up to cover more ground.

Boiling with excitement, Ty reached into his pocket, pulled out his star crystal, and ran into the nearest cave he could find. He zipped through it in no time at all, but the only thing he found inside were a few hairy spiders clinging to the walls. So he bolted out of that cave and into another as quickly as he could. Then another and another. It seemed like they were bouncing from one cave to another all day long, and the only thing they found were bats, rats, and some nasty hairy spiders.

Ty figured that he might have better luck if he could find a real deep cave that leads far below the crystal mountain, so he headed out to find the darkest corner on the farthest side of the crystal mountain. He searched everywhere for a way in, but the walls were too thick to break through and so smooth he couldn't climb up and look for an entrance above.

Ty was determined to find a way in. But just as he was about to head back to find Normack, he walked past a clump of bushes and felt a cool breeze drifting through its branches.

"This has got to be the place," muttered Ty. "There must be a hidden cavern somewhere around here."

He pulled out his sword and started slashing his way through the thick, heavy branches. His heart pounded with excitement; he could feel the cool cave air rushing over him as he slashed his way deeper into the brush. Once he sliced past the last clump of branches, he saw a huge crack in the crystal wall. Peering into the crack, he saw that it led into a magnificent cave with brightly colored walls and columns of stone stretching up to the ceiling. Walking through that huge crack, Ty took his time and looked all around. It looked like nothing had stepped foot inside there for hundreds of years. Ty slid his sword through his belt and headed into the cave with his star crystal in one hand and his shield by his side.

The deeper he got, the more that the walls started to sparkle like stars in the sky, all lit up in the light of his star crystal. But when Ty walked up to get a better look, he stopped dead in his tracks.

"Holy crap," Ty muttered in shock. "These walls are covered with thousands of diamonds, red rubies, and emeralds!"

Ty knew that all the jewels in the world wouldn't be able to help his grandmother at all. He didn't come for diamonds or jewels; he was only interested in finding some blue fire rubies. Even so, Ty was no fool; he still grabbed the biggest and best jewels he could reach and filled his pockets until they bulged. He knew they wouldn't cure his grandma, but they sure would come in handy since his dad wouldn't be able to work until his broken leg healed.

Continuing through the cave, he started to feel the breeze of cold damp air getting stronger and stronger. He knew there had to be another cave that led deeper into the crystal mountain somewhere close. But as he approached the end of the cave, he found a tremendous pile of boulders blocking his way. By the looks of it, Ty knew right away that there must have been a cave-in, and he figured the cave had to keep going on the other side. So he started digging as hard as he could to make his way through the wall of collapsed stone. It was impossible. Those boulders that blocked his way were bigger than a bus and must have weighed tons.

Ty sat down and put his head in his hands trying, to come up with another idea. His heart was broken and he was about to give up and try another cave when he saw a crevice in the ground leading deep into the dark shadows. Its crooked path ran along the back side of that shattered wall and disappeared into the darkness. That cave-in must have broken the floor wide open. When Ty knelt down and looked into that crevice, he could feel the cold air rushing up, and he could see that it led down into another cavern far below the mountain. This is what Ty was looking for—a secret passageway leading under the crystal mountain.

Ty tied his life leech rope to a jagged rock and slid through the crack and started lowering himself down. Kicking off from the sheer wall, he zipped down that crevice and discovered a huge cavern with steep smooth walls dripping with sweet water and a small river flowing across a rocky shore. Wow, what a beautiful place it was. The air was fresh and crisp, not musty and damp like all the others he had explored.

"There must be some blue fire rubies down here somewhere," Ty blurted out. "I can feel it."

Ty was so excited that he started to run along the river's edge, looking up at the walls, trying to spot any flickering sign of blue light coming off those rubies. However, he wasn't paying much attention to where he was running, tripped over a tree root, and fell face-first in the dirt. The sound of his impact echoed throughout the cave. He sat up, rubbing his head and spitting out chunks of dirt. Slamming into the ground like that reminded him real fast that he had better be more careful down here. With a little grin and a quick look around as he stood up, he was so glad that nobody saw him.

Ty brushed the rest of the dirt off his face with his sleeve, held his star crystal up, and started walking more carefully. He looked all around, behind fallen rocks and along the ceiling. He followed that river for miles. When he came up to the end of that cavern, it happened: glowing brightly, high up the rocky cliff wall, he spotted the biggest blue fire ruby that he had ever seen.

"Yahoo!" Ty screamed out with excitement. "I knew I would find some! If I would have kept running, I would have missed it. There must be an angel watching over me today."

Ty was bursting with excitement. He ran straight up to that wall, threw his bow and arrows to the ground, and started to climb. It was the hardest thing he ever tried to climb in his life. The rocky cliff walls were dripping wet and covered with green slippery moss, but he took his time and studied every move he made. Inch by inch, he made his way up that treacherous wall, then when he reached out to grab his treasure, the rock he was holding on to started to pull loose. Ty reached out and latched onto a small lip in the wall just as the rock pulled out and went crashing to the ground below.

"That was too close," muttered Ty.

Then he took a deep breath, reached out, and ripped that huge blue fire ruby out of that wall with his bare hands.

"I've got it. I can't believe it. I finally got one."

Feeling very proud of himself, he climbed down as fast as he could, jumping the rest of the way when he got close to the ground.

Ty stood strong at the bottom of that wall, wiped the sweat off his forehead, and gazed into the glow of that blue fire ruby. He knew right away that it would be more than enough to help his grandmother, and there probably would be enough left over to help his dad.

He walked over to the river's edge and cleaned off the sticky moss and mud, then wrapped it up and put it safely into his pouch. He had a very long trip back home, and he wasn't about to lose it after all he's been through.

CHAPTER 7

The Battle Below

Ty was so proud of what he had accomplished that he started to whistle as he headed back. There was no better feeling in the world than the happiness Ty was feeling right now. He reached down and grabbed a great skipping rock and sent it flying across that underground river. It skipped fourteen times and almost made it all the way across.

"Cool," muttered Ty. "This next one is going to be a record."

So after looking around for a couple of seconds, Ty spotted an awesome skipper. As he reached down to pick it up, an arrow came screaming next to his head and zipped into the river.

"What was that?" screamed Ty as he looked at the water, then back at the walls of the cavern.

Once again, the high-pitched sound of arrows in flight filled the air. "Oh no, you don't!" shouted Ty as he spun around and held up his shield in time to stop three more arrows. *Crack, crack, crack!* The sound echoed in the darkness as they shattered against Ty's shield.

There was no way Ty was going to just stand there being a target, so he stood up boldly and pulled out his sword and shouted as loud as he could, "Whoever is firing these arrows at me had better stop right now and come out, or I'll come in there after you!"

Ty held his sword high, ready for anything. All he could see were dark shadows and huge boulders scattered throughout the cavern floor. All of a sudden, one of those shadows seemed to flinch.

Ty readied his shield and said, "I see you there, hiding behind that rock. If you don't throw down that bow and come out, I'm going to come up there after you and pound you until your head falls off!"

Soft whispers drifted across the cavern floor as a shadowy figure crept between Ty and his only exit.

"Well, are you coming out or do I have to come over there and pull you out?" ordered Ty.

Finally, a tall creature walked out from its hiding place and into the light of the star crystal. Although it walked like a man, it looked more like a lizard. It had big blue eyes and light green scales covering it from head to toe. You could tell it was nervous because its long tail was flicking from side to side.

Ty looked over at that thing and said, "I don't know what your problem is, but if you shoot one more arrow at me, I'll shove it down your throat!"

In a very deep voice, it said, "Thief. You are a thief, and you are trespassing in the caves of the lost souls. My name is Torg, and I am the keeper of the gates of Zintar. You're too small to be a rinog and you don't smell like a Norgon, but you steal the blue stones from us, so you must be working for them."

Ty lowered his shield and said, "I don't know what you are talking about, but if you call me a thief one more time, I am going to break my foot off in your mouth!"

Torg looked at Ty and flicked his tail. "If you are not working for the Norgons, then why did you steal from us? You cannot lie to me! I watched you, with my own eyes, pull the blue stone from the wall and put it in that pouch."

Ty pulled the blue fire ruby out of his pouch and handed it back to Torg. "Do you mean this thing here? Because if you do, I swear I didn't know that it belonged to anybody. In fact, I didn't know that anybody was living in this cave or I would've never come down here. I am not a thief, and I have never stolen anything in my life."

Torg snatched the stone right out of his hands, placed it on the rock shelf behind him, and then waved his hand over his head as if to signal another guard that it was okay.

"You are not welcome here," snapped Torg. "But since you gave it back and did not try to lie about it, I will let you live. Just remember, if you try to return here I will kill you."

Ty couldn't believe his ears. He finally found what he came for, but he had to give it right back. As Ty turned to walk away, he thought he should try at least one time to explain why he needed the stone. So he turned and called out, "Wait a minute, Torg. I traveled a very long way for a blue fire ruby like that one. I desperately need it. Before I leave, I've got to ask. Would you like to trade or barter for it?"

Torg looked at Ty, then flicked his tail. "What kind of trickery are you trying to pull?"

"I swear on my honor, I am not trying to pull any trick on you. If you give me a chance, I'd like to trade what I have for that rock. You don't understand how far I traveled and how badly I need it. Please let me at least show you what I have."

Now Ty was a bit nervous, but he had nothing left to lose. So he reached into his pouch and pulled out some willow bark. "I have some powerful medicine that will ease the pain when you get hurt, and I have some aloe plants that can help heal your wounds."

You could see the look on Torg's face that he wasn't very interested in what Ty had to offer.

"What you offer means nothing to me. I cannot barter with you. So leave now before I change my mind."

"Wait, I have more to trade. I even have some precious gems that I found in the cavern above. You can have them all."

Torg just shook his head and pointed toward the way Ty came in. Ty looked around and checked his pockets, and the only thing he had left was a couple of those apples that he had picked right before he met Normack and a handful of berries.

"You can have these too. They are sweet apples and berries that I picked myself. I'm sorry, but this is all I have left. If it's not enough, I will give you my sword and shield too. Please, Torg, it's all that I have."

Torg's eyes opened wide and his voice started to shake. "This is what you are offering in trade?" Torg looked at Ty and said, "My job is to protect the gates of Zintar and all that belongs to it. I do not have the right to trade what does not belong to me, but I will take your offer to the one who can. Stay here and do not move, and I will return with your answer."

Ty kept his fingers crossed as he watched Torg walk away and disappear into the shadows on the far side of that cavern. While Ty waited, the cave seemed to come alive with whispers and hushed voices. The longer he stood there, the more he noticed the creatures sneaking around in the shadows. It was starting to become a little creepy just standing there. After a few minutes, he saw Torg approaching from deep inside the cave, and he wasn't alone. There were four others with him.

Torg walked right up to Ty and told him to bow his head because he was in the presence of Her Majesty Queen Lylah, ruler of Zintar. It was very easy to figure out who Torg was talking about. Queen Lylah was a beautiful young girl draped in a long bright red robe and wearing three thick necklaces made of solid gold. Ty did just what he was told and bowed his head in respect.

Then Ty looked over at Torg and asked, "What did I do to be honored with a visit from Her Majesty Queen Lylah?"

That was when Queen Lylah explained softly, "We do not get many visitors here. The ones that do venture to our lands are usually thieves and raiders that try to steal our treasures. My royal guardian told me that he watched you from the shadows as you took a stone that did not belong to you. Then he informed me, as you were trying to escape, he shot in order to protect my kingdom, but you did not shoot back. Instead, you returned the stone immediately and asked to trade for it. Is that true?"

"Yes, it is all true, except he forgot to tell you that I didn't know that anyone lived here. I am not looking for a fight or to steal from anybody. I am just on a quest for my family."

Queen Lylah spoke out once more in her soft voice, "What you have offered us in payment for this stone is unacceptable. We could never make such a deal with you."

Ty was so disappointed he nearly started to cry. "I have nothing left to offer you of value. You see, that blue fire ruby that I found is the only thing that will help my grandmother recover from her illness, so I will offer you anything if you would find it in your heart to trade with me."

Queen Lylah looked proudly at Ty and said, "I can see that you are an honorable and noble creature, but there is no way I would ever trade that ruby for what you are offering."

She raised her hand and two huge guards lumbered out from the deep shadows of the cave, dragging a large black sack behind them, big enough that he could probably fit inside and tie up the top.

"Although those shiny stones are pretty, we have no need for them. You may have them back. But the willow, aloe, and fresh fruit you have offered are worth so much more than this small piece of a blue fire ruby. I will, in turn, give you this sack of blue fire rubies in trade for what you have offered. That is, if you still wish to barter with me."

Ty's jaw dropped to the ground in disbelief. There were more blue fire rubies in that sack than he had ever seen before. Its sides bulged out while the brittle sounds of crystals clinking together rang out as the guards placed it gently by his feet. Queen Lylah looked right into Ty's eyes and told him, "My people are of noble blood. To accept your great offer for just one small ruby would, too, be like stealing. I would like to make this deal fair for you and my people."

Ty was speechless; all he could do was stand there with his mouth hanging open. It was so unbelievable. There was enough in that sack to help his whole village for a very long time. In fact, there was enough in that sack to keep his village going while they fixed the cave at Eagle Cliff that collapsed.

"Thank you, thank you, thank you," Ty muttered. "Thank you very much. You have no idea how wonderful this is. You have saved my grandmother's life and my village with your generosity."

Queen Lylah clapped her hands and said, "The deal is done. I will send one of my guardians with you. He will guard you and he will carry and protect this sack with his life. There is only one thing you must know. I will only allow my guard to go with you as far as the opening to the caves of the lost souls. Then he must return and you will be on your own."

Ty told Queen Lylah that he thought sending one of her royal guardians to protect him was a great thing to do, and when he got to the clearing outside, his friend would be there and together they would be just fine. Ty couldn't stop thanking Queen Lylah for all she had done and vowed that he would return someday with a feast for her and her people in thanks for what she has done.

Queen Lylah smiled and held out her hand. "Take this ring. It holds the royal seal of Zintar if you so choose to return. All you have to do is show my guardian this ring. You will be protected from any harm and be treated as my royal guest."

Ty bowed his head and thanked her once more, then turned and started to make his way back to the surface with the prize of a lifetime.

"Wait, Ty, do not forget your pretty stones," Torg said in his deep voice. "You said they were special to you, so do not forget them."

Ty turned back and blushed a little bit. "I almost forgot. I did want to give them to my mom and dad. They would love to have them."

Torg bent down, scooped them up, and gently filled Ty's pouch. "Then they should have them. Now let's go. We have stayed here by the river too long already. The Norgon do not like to pass up an easy target, and we are in one of their hunting grounds."

CHAPTER 8

Surprise In The Darkness

Ty was bursting with excitement. He had more blue fire rubies than he could have possibly wished for.

Torg turned to Queen Lylah and said, "With your permission, since this creature acted with respect and honor toward me, I wish to serve as his protector and join your guardian in carrying out your wishes that he safely arrives with the stones to the caves of lost souls."

Queen Lylah nodded her head, granting Torg's wishes, and chose her strongest guardian, Scales, to carry the sack of blue fire rubies.

Torg couldn't help but smile. The other guardian was his good buddy. Now Scales was quite a bit bigger than Torg, and he had this long scar across his face from a battle against a Norgon war lord. All the Zintarian guards knew and respected him because he was one of the toughest and meanest guardians to ever wear the mark of the queen's personal guards.

Scales smiled a little bit, snatched the sack of rubies right off the ground with one hand, slung it over his shoulder with a rattling thud, then stepped proudly beside Torg and stood at attention. "I am honored to go, my queen. I will carry your gift proudly and protect it as you commanded."

Then Torg and Scales knelt on one knee respectfully to Queen Lylah, stood back up, and turned to walk away.

Scales looked back at Ty with a grin on his face. "Are you coming?"

Ty turned back to Queen Lylah, bowed deeply, and smiled, saying, "Thank you again, Your Majesty. I will never forget your kindness."

All three headed along the river's edge and disappeared back into the darkness. Even though Ty had two strong guardians to lead him back through the cavern, it was still a bit creepy there with the flutter of bats flying high in the cavern and the sound of the river splashing against the rocky shore.

Scales took the lead, and Torg walked a few paces behind him. They were marching like true soldiers, stride for stride, in perfect step. As they made their way deeper into the cavern, Ty couldn't figure out how they knew which way to go, but somehow, they did. It really didn't bother him too much because he was headed out with his prize, and at the pace they were going, he would be back outside in no time at all.

As they walked along the shore of that underground river, Ty was so happy that he started to pick up some stones and hurl them across the river while humming a little marching song in the rhythm of their steps.

"What do you think you are doing?" asked Torg. "You're making such a big racket. Every creature around is going to hear us coming."

"What are you worried about? There's nothing around down here but bats and spiders."

"Hush up, you two," whispered Scales. "I don't want to break up your conversation, but you guys had better quiet down. Those two pillars of iron ore over there mark the edge of the Norgons' territory, and I don't feel like fighting off an army right now."

"Wait just one minute," said Ty. "Torg didn't say anything about Norgons before. What's a Norgon? What do you mean about fighting off an army?"

Scales stopped, turned to Ty, and explained. "Norgons are vicious creatures that travel in packs, just like wolfs. They live by scavenging and plundering anything they can get their claws on. It is hard to hear them coming because they ride on the backs of wild cave rats. I have fought them many times. They are strong and very sneaky. I have seen the scattered bits of flesh and bones after an attack. The lucky ones are killed by spears or arrows while the ones that survive are fed to their pets."

"They ride rats? What do these things look like?"

Torg looked over at Ty and tried to explain, "You do not understand, Ty. A full-grown Norgon warrior could stand four or five feet tall. They have incredibly thick armor and a nasty attitude to go with it. If that's not bad enough, they look more like huge flying insects, almost like a huge praying mantis, with poisonous spikes on their backs and arms and large eyes like that of a fly. They are hard to kill, and they never stop attacking even after you hack off a couple of their legs. Now do you understand? We should move quickly now and keep quiet!"

Ty didn't say another word. He just nodded his head and grasped his sword tightly. He remembered his last encounter with a cave rat, and they were nothing to play around with.

Torg looked at Scales and said, "Considering you are carrying that heavy sack, you should take the rear and I'll take the lead. That way we will be able to move quickly if anything happens."

Ty pushed his way ahead and interrupted them sharply, "Listen, you two. I didn't see a thing when I walked through here earlier. I don't think there are any of these Norgon around anywhere. So let's just keep going."

But it was a bit too late. Their voices had already echoed throughout the cave and caught the attention of a rogue Norgon scout. It crept silently above their heads, across a rocky ledge, studying their every move.

Fortunately, this Norgon scout was very young and alone. It didn't dare attack. It stayed in the shadows, waiting and watching.

Torg and Scales were unaware that they were being watched, but they knew that this was a very dangerous place, so they stayed alert and cautious as they walked along the trail that Ty left when he first got there. Meanwhile, slowly closing in on them from behind was a squad of Norgon warriors with one thing on their mind—food.

Torg and Scales weren't guardians of Zintar for nothing. They were sharp and courageous warriors trained from birth for combat.

Scales stopped right where he was and gripped his spear tightly, whispering, "Shhhh, I think I hear something."

"I think I hear something too," whispered Ty as he crouched down low, studying the shadows behind them. "It sounds like it's coming from back there."

Torg and Scales looked at each other with dark and determined eyes. Quickly, Scales looked around and pointed to the cavern's wall. In a flash, he tossed the sack of blue fire rubies behind a stone pillar and started to wipe their tracks clean while Torg led Ty to a safe hiding spot right behind a large crystal pillar jutting out from the ground next to the wall.

"Here they come, Torg," whispered Scales, pointing into the shadows. "Get him down." Then just as the Norgons came into sight, Scales finished covering their tracks, dove behind the pillar, and drew his bow.

"We will stay hidden right here, Ty," said Torg, "and wait for them to pass us by, but if we have to fight, this will be a good place to defend ourselves."

It didn't take long until Ty had his first look at a Norgon warrior. There must have been a dozen of them scurrying along the shoreline, riding on the backs of the biggest cave rats he had ever seen while a dozen foot soldiers followed close behind.

"They look like some kind of evil aliens," whispered Ty. "I hope they don't see us. All I want to do is get back home. I don't want to fight those things."

"We will get you home," muttered Torg defiantly. "We just have to hide out here for a little while until those things move off."

Torg, Scales, and Ty watched as the hunting party stopped right below them and jumped off those nasty beasts. The cave rats had leathery saddles strapped to their backs and thick chains around their necks for the Norgon to use as reins to control them.

Torg tried as hard as he could to keep Ty safely hidden, but he just kept peeking around the side of that pillar to watch them as they scurried around the shoreline, trying to pick up their trail. They buzzed and clicked like locusts to each other while they stabbed their spears furiously into the water as if they had seen something in its wake.

When the three Norgons that were riding the biggest rats in the back of the pack finally arrived, they stood around in the center of the beach, looking around, studying everything in sight. After a few minutes, the largest one—with a big chunk of its right claw missing—reached out and waived its spear high above its head and made a terrible screech.

It took only seconds until Ty figured out what that thing had meant as the foot soldiers ran back and released the rats they had chained down. Scales must have known what that thing was doing too because he grabbed Ty by his shoulder to pull him back into the shadows safely behind him and Torg.

"Stay very quiet and very still," whispered Scales. "They're releasing their rats to hunt us down. If they do not hear us or pick up our scent, they should leave soon. I scattered some Ava root across our tracks. That should keep us safe."

Torg, Scales, and Ty stayed hunkered down in the shadows, not making a single sound. Ty's heart started pounding as he remembered how scared he was when his father told him wild stories about the Shadow Forest. Then suddenly, a quiet calm flowed through Ty's body and he was no longer scared. He knew that he didn't want to fight, but he was ready to fight if he had to; his fear was gone. He started to become a true warrior.

They calmly watched in silence as those rats scurried in all directions. Back and forth they went, sniffing and scratching the rocky shoreline for any fresh scent. Ty clenched his sword tightly as he watched one start digging where he once had stood. Squealing and hopping madly, it shoved its nose deep into the ground as two more rats joined it, ripping apart the area.

Scales and Torg kept tapping each other, pointing and nodding, watching and planning as the Norgons fanned out in their desperate search.

The Norgons and their disgusting rats scoured the whole beach from the water's edge to the cavern's wall, but they never picked up any sign of our friends.

Scales knew his trick had worked as that hunting party started to gather back at the river's edge. Then with a loud screech, one of the leaders jumped on its rat and started to ride back where they came from. Scales and Torg lowered their bows and let out a soft sigh of relief.

However, their luck had just run out. That lone scout that was hiding above their heads stood up and let out the most awful screech you've ever heard, then pointed right at them, giving their position away.

"So much for hiding, Torg!" yelled Scales. "I prefer to do this the old-fashioned way: shoot first and then shoot again."

Torg let out a fiercely powerful growl, then stood up and sent an arrow screeching through the air. *Smack!* His arrow sank deep into its target, sending that creature tumbling off its rat and into the rushing water. The whole cavern lit up with the sounds of Norgons screeching and scurrying to find cover.

Zip, zip, zip! The Norgon fired back with slings and poison-tipped arrows. They smacked against the crystal pillar and shattered like glass.

"Watch out!" screamed Torg, knocking Ty to the ground as an arrow sliced by his head. "If you get the smallest scratch from one of those arrows, you will be dead in seconds."

Shot after shot, Torg and Scales kept the hordes of vicious monsters back. However, they didn't come prepared for a ferocious battle against a whole squad of Norgon warriors. They were running out of arrows fast.

Ty, tired of staying out of the fight, grabbed his bow and sent an arrow screaming down and slamming into a Norgon's head, just as it was getting ready to fire again.

"I said get down and stay down!" yelled Torg. "Remember, it's my job to make sure you leave here in one piece, and I'm going to do just that."

"Are you kidding?" shouted Ty. "You're totally outnumbered and you need my help. If I don't start helping soon, we all won't make it out of here alive. Now stand back and watch this!"

Quick as lightning, Ty drew another arrow and fired his bow, sinking the arrow deep into the chest of a charging cave rat. Shot after shot, those three kept fighting as the Norgons continued their attack.

"I'm almost out of arrows," shouted Scales.

"Me too," said Torg as he dove out of the way, landing behind a small boulder, as another arrow nearly hit him in his throat.

"My arrows are useless against those Norgons' thick armor," screamed Ty. "We've got to make a break for it soon before we get surrounded."

Scales knew they would never survive if they tried to run. Those Norgons moved too fast riding on those greasy cave rats, and there was no cover to hide behind for at least one hundred yards. They had no choice. They had to fight it out right now before that lone scout could return with more troops.

"Are you guys ready," shouted Ty? "I'm getting real tired of these jokers trying to kill us. So grab your swords and follow me 'cause it's payback time."

Ty sent his last arrow into the heart of a rat, dropped his bow, drew his sword, and gripped his shield. He wasn't about to take it anymore. It was go time. With a thunderous battle cry that echoed throughout the cave, Ty charged out from behind that crystal pillar and headed straight for three Norgon warriors. Blocking arrows with his shield and jumping across two dead cave rats, he slashed his way into the heart of the Norgon's army.

Torg and Scales were right behind him, chopping and hacking their way across the cave, pushing any Norgon warrior that was left into the freezing cold river.

Ty, Scales, and Torg fought like a hurricane ripping through a forest of paper trees—moving across the cave and attacking every warrior in sight until the last one fell.

Torg looked over at Ty and said, "You fight like a true guardian, but remember, if anybody is going to give the order to charge, it'll be me, and don't ever forget that!" Then turning to Scales, he added, "Now that's the last of them. We better get out of here right now before more start coming. I'll pick up some of these arrows and you grab the rubies, and then let's get going."

Scales looked back at Ty and whispered softly over his shoulder to Torg, "That kid's got guts, Commander."

"You're right, and if he tries another stunt like that again, we might get a chance to see them lying across the ground!" he replied in a low, sarcastic tone.

"Young warrior," snapped Torg as he walked over the body of a rat. "Hurry now and grab as many arrows as you can, and be careful not to scratch yourself. After a fight like that, I would hate to lose you because you were careless. Grab yourself one of their bows too. The one next to that leader should prove to be an improvement over that stick of yours!"

Ty nodded his head and started running around, picking up as many arrows as he could find. They knew that if the word got out where they were, they would need all the arrows they could carry. Scales charged back to the cavern's wall, snatched that sack of rubies from behind the pillar, and threw it over his shoulder. "Let's go! Move it! Move it! Move it!" Torg shouted out, like a drill sergeant to his troops. "We've already stayed here too long!"

CHAPTER 9

The Attack Of The Rinog

It was amazing how quickly they made it back to where Ty's rope was hanging. When Torg and Scales saw that rope hanging there, they stopped right in their tracks.

Torg looked over at Ty, then shook his head. "Zintarians can't climb ropes, but don't worry. We're the best climbers in Zintar. We'll climb up the cliff face instead."

Ty just smiled and shook his head, realizing that, since those two were part lizard, climbing straight up a cavern wall should be no big deal for them.

"No problem," Ty admitted as he looked at their razor-sharp claws. "I think it would be much easier and a lot safer if we just tie the sack of blue fire rubies to the end of my rope and pull it up to the top when we get there."

"Yes, I agree," Torg admitted and then tied the satchel tightly to the end of the rope. "We'll help pull it up after you climb up. It shouldn't take too long."

Ty looked around and started to get that sneaky little grin on his face again. You could tell right away that he was up to something.

"Hey, you guys, I bet you I can make it to the top before you two can."

"Only a fool would bet a Zintarian to a climbing race!" laughed Scales, slapping Torg across his back.

"Oh, are you scared that you'll be defeated?" replied Ty with a smirk from ear to ear.

"You're on," said Torg as his tail flicked anxiously. "And if we win, you must carry the sack all the way out to the opening of the caves of the lost souls while we escort you."

"Okay, you got it. The loser carries the bag for the rest of the way."

Ty wanted to beat those two to the top of the cave real bad. He figured he would have a real good chance because they had a longer way to go, and it was going to be a really hard climb, even for them.

"Get ready, set, and go," yelled Scales.

"Holy smokes!" Ty muttered as he watched those two take off running across the cave, disappearing in a wisp of dust. "Those two are super fast!"

Ty jumped over the sack, snatched the rope, and started to climb as fast as he could. When he was about halfway up, Ty peeked over at Torg and Scales and couldn't believe what he saw. They weren't having any problems climbing up that cave wall at all. In fact, they looked like a couple of squirrels running up a tree. The race was definitely on.

Ty wasn't about to give up now. He wanted to show those guys that he was a strong warrior too. He knew he had an edge on those two, not because he the best rope climber in school but because those guys had to race across the floor, then up the wall and finally make their way to that skinny opening.

Ty pulled and pulled as hard as he could. He climbed so hard his hands started to turn red and his arms started to burn. Before long, he reached the top of the cliff and started to wiggle and pull his way through the jagged crack in the floor. With his muscles burning and his hands throbbing, Ty spun around, grabbed the rope, and started to pull that heavy sack up.

Torg and Scales must have had some trouble coming up because Ty had that sack safely on the ground next to him, and they still weren't anywhere around. So he grabbed his rope, coiled it back up, and slung it around his shoulder.

Totally exhausted, Ty sat down on the edge of the cliff and swung his feet over the side, giggling with excitement. He knew that he beat the pants off those two. With every muscle in his body burning like fire, he just sat there, resting, barely able to move at all. After a few seconds, Ty felt one of them reach down and pick up the sack behind him.

"What happened to you two? I thought you guys would have been here already," laughed Ty as he flipped a rock down the hole. "Now which one of you guys are going to carry my sack the rest of the way out?"

When Ty looked over his shoulder and saw Scales and Torg running right toward him from the back of the cave, with their bows in their hands, he gasped and froze in shock.

"Get down, Ty! Get down!" screamed Scales.

"What in the world is going on here?" said Ty, standing up and spinning around. He found himself face-to-face with a huge rinog. Softly, he muttered, "Hey now, big fella, I don't want any trouble. But that's my sack you have in your hands and you're not leaving here with it. So please give it back."

Just as soon as the last word left his mouth, that big thing reached back and clobbered Ty so hard he flew all the way across the cave and smashed into the wall on the other side.

Torg and Scales sent their arrows screeching through the cave right at that rinog's chest. *Smack! Smack!* You could hear the sound echoing across the cave as they hit their mark. They fired again and again, but their arrows only smashed against its thick gray hide.

"Get behind me, Ty," yelled Torg. "I will protect you!"

Ty lay there a little dazed for a few seconds and then slowly sat up. It was amazing that horrendous punch didn't kill him, but his armor was strong and that hit only made him mad. He reached back, drew an arrow, and fired. You could hear the loud crack ring out as Ty's arrow hit that rinog right in the back of its head.

"I told you that I didn't want any trouble, but if you think you're going to leave here with my stuff, you've got another thing coming!" yelled Ty, sending another screaming across the cavern.

I guess that rinog wanted that sack really bad because it let out a terrible roar and charged with all its might. Ty stood up, clenched his fists, and then slung his bow back over his shoulder. "If you think you're man enough, then bring it on!"

Torg and Scales couldn't believe their eyes. Nobody had ever survived a fight against a rinog before. Everyone knows that only a full-grown vipercon would have a chance against a charging rinog.

"Don't just stand there," yelled Torg. "You must get out of there and climb as high as you can. We'll try to distract it. Now go."

Ty heard the whistle of arrows screaming by and smashing right into that rinog's neck, but they were just snapping like twigs.

"Run, Ty. Get out of there!" Scales hollered.

Ty just stood his ground, not flinching an inch. Closer and closer, that huge beast came. The ground started to shake, and pieces of the rock walls were starting to crumble to the ground.

"Look out!" screamed Torg.

But it was too late; that rinog was running full blast, and it was just a few feet away from pounding a mudhole in Ty.

Just as it lowered its head, Ty sprung into action. Fast as lightning, Ty grabbed that monster by its ears and flipped him over his shoulder, sending it hurtling across the cave. The rinog let out a tremendous roar as it sailed through the air.

"Watch out, Scales!" screamed Torg as he tumbled out of the way seconds before it slammed into the crystal pillars they were standing by. It hit with a mighty crash, sending large chunks of rock and crystals flying everywhere.

Ty jumped on top of a busted-up piece of crystal and shouted out, "How do you like being tossed across a cave? It kind of hurts, doesn't it? Now drop that sack right now and get out of here, or I'm going to teach you a lesson about stealing that you'll never forget!"

Torg watched in amazement as a cloud of rock dust swirled across the floor as that rinog lay flat on its face. It lay there dazed for a minute, then struggled as it tried to stand. When it looked over at Ty, the veins in its huge arms started to throb and its gray face turned beet red with fury.

"Well, what are you waiting for?" shouted Ty. "Are you going to put my stuff down, or do you want some more?"

That was all it could stand. It went into a furious rage. With a deafening roar, it charged right at Ty, swinging wildly, pounding massive stone columns into dust as it closed in on Ty.

Scales and Torg kept shooting their bows, trying to give Ty time to get away from that rinog's deadly rampage. But Ty just stood there again, watching as it got closer and closer. He knew it was no use trying to run, so he readied his shield and pulled out his sword, smiling at that rinog because, this time, he was ready for battle.

With an explosion that rocked the cave, they clashed head-on. Dust was flying and the walls were shaking as Ty went hand-to-hand with him. All you could see were glimpses of Ty swinging his sword and blocking that beast's mighty blows with his shield as a cloud of dust rolled across the floor.

Torg threw down his bow, then grabbed his knife and dove right into that fight. But Torg never stood a chance; he had no armor or shield to protect him.

He pounced on that rinog's back and grabbed it by its horn. While pulling back as hard as he could, he slammed his blade into its neck, but its hide was so thick it didn't even leave a scratch.

"Let go of him, you jerk, or I'll rip your head off!" screamed Torg, throwing his knife to the ground and grabbing it with both hands.

Its head flung back as Torg strained with all his might.

"I've got him. Grab the rubies, Scales!" shouted Torg.

But Scales was too busy joining the fight. He dove into the dust-filled air headfirst, landing on its chest, grabbed its arm, and started prying it back. Fuming with anger, it let out a tremendous roar, drew back its fist, and clobbered Scales with a lucky shot, sending him flying and tumbling across the floor and over the edge of the cliff.

"No!" Torg screamed as he turned and watched his friend disappear into the blackness.

Seconds later, the hollow sound of Scales's body slamming into the ground at the bottom of the cliff echoed across the floor like a cold winter's wind.

Torg let go of that rinog's horn with one hand and started punching it in the face as hard as he could.

When that rinog realized that Torg had let go with one hand, it swung its head around and bashed him with his horn, sending Torg across the room and into a crystal pillar. His body flopped to the ground, all twisted and still.

Ty was furious and lost all control. He threw his shield down in the dirt, and with his sword held high, he charged at that rinog in a screaming blind rage.

The rinog kicked up a wave of dust as it lowered its head and charged back at Ty. The only ones left standing were seconds away from a devastating impact.

Ty leaped into the air and came down on that rinog's head with a mighty chop from his sword. *Smack!* But Ty's attack wasn't enough to slow it down one bit.

That rinog unleashed his fury and slammed into Ty with the force of a freight train. It dug its horn deep across Ty's chest and smashed him so hard he flew across the cave, hit the ceiling, and came crashing to the floor below.

Ty and Torg were both lying face-first in the dirt, covered with dirt and busted rock, motionless and barely breathing.

The rinog let out a hideous growl, standing there, gazing down at our two friends as the dust swirled across the floor.

It took a few moments until they could open their eyes, dazed and seeing stars. After a knockdown drag-out fight like that, neither one could move at all, all they could do was lie there helplessly and watch as the rinog ran away and disappeared into the blackness with his prize.

Ty rolled over, shook Torg, and mumbled, "Scales. We got to help Scales!"

With every ounce of energy, they crawled back to the edge of the ravine and looked down. Scales was lying there, all busted up on a pile of rocks. "Is he dead?" Ty whispered.

"No, he can't be. He can't be dead. He's just knocked out or something."

Torg didn't bother going back to the side of the cliff to climb down safely; he just reached over and dug his claws into the cold, hard stone and slid down, leaving a jagged line of claw marks in the stone wall. Then Ty flung his rope over the edge and followed Torg down.

"Scales, get up," ordered Torg. "You can't let that thing beat you. I won't allow it!"

Torg bent down and gently turned Scales over. He was still breathing. "Did you get the rubies back?" mumbled Scales as blood dripped from the corner of his mouth. "Is Ty all right?"

"Ty's fine. He right here. But that rinog got away with the blue fire rubies."

"You've got to get them back, Torg. The queen, she was counting on us."

"Don't worry, my friend. I'll get them back. Can you make it back to Zintar?"

Scales slowly sat up and leaned against the wall. "Yes, yes. I'll be all right. Now go and get them back. That's an order."

"Let's go," barked Torg.

"Are you nuts? We can't just leave him here like this. Forget the rubies. We got to help Scales."

"I'll be okay, Ty. I've had worse falls than that when I was young. So just get going, and, Torg, I will inform the queen that you will not be returning until Ty's gift is back safely in his hands. Now go, the both of you, and may the winds of luck be with you!"

Torg and Ty nodded their heads in silence and started to climb back up. This time, they went very slowly as they struggled inch by inch, their bodies weak and battered. But they kept on climbing and climbing.

Finally, they struggled to pull themselves over the edge of the wall and collapsed on the ground, exhausted and gasping for breath. A few minutes passed, and then Ty looked over at Torg, took a deep breath, and asked, "Where in the world did that thing come from, and could you please explain to me how it was able to walk right up behind me without making a sound?"

"I don't know where it came from, but rinogs are known for their stealth when they hunt. What I want to know is, what in the world were you thinking of challenging a full-grown rinog to a fight? Are you nuts?"

Ty just smiled. "At least I had my sword and my armor to protect me. When you jumped on that rinog's back with a dull knife, I thought you must be either the bravest person I've ever known or the stupidest one ever born."

"You think that was stupid?" Torg laughed. "Now tell me, just what in the world were you thinking when you challenged it to a fight in the first place? You know the only thing that could stop a rinog is a vipercon."

"I'm not an idiot. I know only a vipercon can bring down a rinog, but I sure can slow it down, and if you don't believe me, then maybe you can explain how I got its blood on my sword."

"What, let me see that," Torg sputtered. "How could that be? That's not possible. No weapon ever created has ever cut a rinog! You must have cut yourself."

Ty laughed. "I didn't cut myself. My blood is red, not blue. I hit that thing with all my might, but all I could do was scratch him up a little bit."

"I vowed to help you get your stuff back, but I don't want to get killed, so next time you feel like picking a fight, why don't you pick on something only twice your size?" snickered Torg as he slapped him on his back. "Now if you're done bragging, we got to get moving before that thing gets away."

"Just try to relax," Ty told him. "I'm not too worried about that monster getting away. As big as that thing is, we won't have any problem tracking it down. The first thing we have to do when we get out of here is find my friend and tell him what happened. Then we can go after that thief and get my stuff back. Trust me, when you meet Normack, you'll understand why that thing won't stand a chance!"

They stood up, knocked the dirt off themselves, and started the long walk out.

Torg looked over at Ty and asked, "Have you thought about what we are going to do when we catch up with that rinog? I mean, do you have a plan on how we are going to get that sack away from him?"

Ty just shrugged his shoulders and said, "I have no idea. I'm just making it up as I go along. Hey, Torg, I think that's the entrance to the cave up ahead. I never thought I would be so glad to get outside. Just look at that beautiful sunlight, so warm and bright."

CHAPTER 10

The Alliance Is Complete

Ty had to cover his eyes as he left the cave. The sun was stunningly bright, and it took awhile for his eyes to get used to it. Torg, on the other hand, had to take it kind of slow since he lived all his life deep underground and the only light he knew came from star crystals. He had to stay in the shadows of the cave for a few minutes longer while his eyes adjusted.

"Now come on out here," Ty said. "The sun feels great."

"This is incredible," Torg said as he walked into the sunlight.

"I've heard stories about the outside, but I never thought it could be so huge and beautiful. How big is this cave you call outside?" Torg asked. "I can't even see any walls, and where is the ceiling?"

"There are no walls or ceilings out here. That is why it is called the outside. You have a lot to learn, my friend," Ty replied.

Torg was spellbound at everything he could see. Ty taught him about the trees and grass, the clouds, and the sky. The world was full of wonder and beauty that Torg had never seen before. It was like showing the world to a child for the first time.

"This is my world," said Ty. "There are more creatures and animals out here than you could possibly imagine. So be careful and watch your step."

As they walked around the side of the crystal mountain, Ty was showing Torg the birds and small creatures that lived all around them.

"I don't believe it." Ty stopped and said, "Would you look at that? While we were in that deep, dark cave, fighting Norgons and getting slammed by a rinog, Normack was just lying around up here getting a sun tan."

Torg looked all around and turned to Ty with a puzzled look on his face. "I don't see anybody anywhere."

"He's right over there, all coiled up like a little baby next to that boulder that kind of looks like a hammer. Hey, sleepyhead, wake up. I want to introduce you to a friend of mine!" Ty shouted.

Normack slowly raised his head, then looked over to Ty and said, "It's about time you got back from that cave, fish feet. I thought you got lost down there. Now where's your little friend that you want me to meet?"

When Torg looked over and got a good look at who Ty was talking to, his eyes opened wide with fear; he didn't know if he should run or fight.

"I don't believe it, Ty. You've got to be kidding me!" muttered Torg as he slowly started to back away. "Please tell me that you are not talking about that vipercon over there?"

"Well, sure I am," laughed Ty. "He's a real good guy once you get to know him, just as long as he doesn't try to eat you like he tried to eat me the first time we met. But don't worry. Since he ate a big cave rat a little while ago, I don't think you will have anything to worry about. Just do yourself a favor and don't get too close to him because his breath could kill a rinog from thirty feet away."

"Well then, if he is a friend of yours, then he's a friend of mine."

Then Torg put down his bow, worked up some courage, and introduced himself to Normack, face-to-face.

"You were in that cave all morning, Ty. I was afraid you might have gotten lost. What in the world were you doing in there for all that time? Did you find any fire rubies?"

"Normack, you got to believe me. It was incredible. I had enough blue fire rubies to help everybody in my whole village," Ty said. "But we ran into a problem, a real nasty problem."

That's when Ty told him the whole story about Queen Lylah, Torg, and Scales and what that rinog did with his rubies.

Normack stood straight up and said, "That must have been the same rinog that came bursting out of the cave about half an hour ago. I don't know what you two did to that thing, but it ran out of that cave so fast I nearly shed my skin. He went over that hill next to those cliffs, heading straight for the lost meadows. It shouldn't be too hard to find him because he was knocking down anything that stood in his way."

Torg jumped up and drew his sword. "What are you two waiting for? That stinking slimeball is trying to get away, and I would like to teach that brute a lesson about stealing that he'll never forget."

"Sounds great to me," hissed Normack, looking back at Torg.

Ty looked around with a huge smile on his face. "Well, guys, the schools are open, and I don't think a note from the teacher is going to be enough. So let's catch up to that jerk and take back what he stole, and if he don't like it, well, I guess he's in for the pounding of his life."

Torg knelt on one knee and drew an arrow on the ground surrounded by some weird symbols.

"Okay," Torg said, walking back to where they were standing. "I am ready now. Let's get going."

"What was that all about?" Ty asked.

"I needed to leave a message for Scales in case he tries to follow us. This will let him know where we are going and what we plan to do."

"Whatever," said Ty. "If you're done playing in the sand, I have some payback to dish out and we are losing daylight."

Nobody said a word as they turned and followed that trail deep into the Shadow Forest. This was the first time in history that anyone had ever tried to track down a full-grown rinog. Ty and Torg both knew, deep down in their souls, that they were lucky to be alive after that pounding they got inside the cave, but to survive a second battle would take a lot more than luck.

"Let's try to pick up some speed," said Torg. "That monster had at least a good hour head start and is probably miles away from us right now."

"That's probably true," Ty said. "But I have a great idea how we can find out for sure. Hey, Normack, can you slither up to the top of those trees and try to see how far that thing might be? If he starts heading toward the valley, we might be able to cut him off by crossing over those hills up ahead."

"That sounds like a great idea," answered Normack and slithered straight up a large tree next to the trail, disappearing into the branches of that tree like a whisper in the night. You couldn't hear a sound, not even the crackle of a single leaf.

"Your friend moves like a ghost," Torg said. "But even for him, it's going to take awhile to make it up to the top of that tree."

"You're right about that," Ty said. "While we wait, do you mind if I ask you something?"

"No, not at all. What do you want to know?"

"Well, I was just kind of curious about what you think of the outside so far."

"Are you kidding?" Torg said. "Your world out here is so amazing! I just don't understand why those creatures invade our caves and smash our homes like they do. We never go to the surface and try to destroy their world. That's why I don't understand why it has attacked my people for all these years. You have seen our world. It isn't full of beautiful riches as far as your eyes can see like your world is."

"Well, Torg, I don't know why those things have been troubling your people for all those years, but it's going to stop as soon as I can get my hands on him. He's going to wish he had never gone into that cave," Ty boasted. "Well, Normack is coming back down. I hope he has some good news."

"How in the world do you know that?" Torg said.

"Well, it's pretty easy," laughed Ty. "The stench of dead rats is getting closer."

"That's not very funny," whispered Normack from the branches just above their heads. "I need you two to listen very closely because I have some bad news. I know which way that rinog is headed. Grab your weapons and prepare yourselves for battle because you're not going to like where it is headed."

CHAPTER 11

The Chase Is On

After all Ty had been through, there wasn't anything at all that was going to scare him now. So he checked his sword and shield, looked at Torg and Normack, and then smiled. Normack was well aware that whenever he smiled like that, you knew it meant trouble. If that rinog knew what was good for him, he would drop that sack and disappear into the forest before those three caught up to him.

Ty walked up to Normack and placed his hand on his side. "Whatever it is, I'm sure it won't be that bad. Wherever it's gone couldn't possibly be worse than the places that we have been. So don't keep it a secret, tell us."

"You don't understand!" Normack shouted, sliding down and coiling up next to him. "That rinog is still about a half hour ahead of us and crushing everything in its path. He's headed straight for a village next to a river, and unfortunately, that village is surrounded by a hedge of razor bushes.

"No, it can't be!" screamed Ty, raising his arm and pointing the other way. "You must be wrong! My village must be miles from here and in that direction. This can't be true!"

Normack raised straight up and shouted, "Look, the crystal mountains is to the north and the swamps are to the east, which must mean that we have traveled in a huge circle. We are almost back to the place where you started. That thing is headed straight for your home, and there is nothing in its way to stop it."

"Normack, we got to stop that thing before it reaches my home. They won't stand a chance! I need your help," begged Ty. "I'm not fast enough to catch up with that rinog before he gets to my village. Please carry me on your back. I know I promised never to ask that again, but without your help, I'll never make it back in time. You can make it there faster than I ever could. Please, Normack, help me save my village."

"You want to ride on my back like a horse? I am a vipercon, lord of the Shadow Forest, and I don't give piggyback rides," hissed Normack in a furious rage.

Ty was crushed as he looked around in despair.

Normack glanced over at Torg, then slowly lowered his head, slithered right up to Ty, and whispered, "Since you have risked your life for me and you have fought to protect others, I would be honored to give you a lift across this treacherous land. Regrettably, I am afraid that it still wouldn't work because your arms are too short and you would fall off and get killed if I traveled fast as the wind."

Ty stood there for a moment because he knew that Normack was right. That's when Ty got a great idea. He took out his sword and sliced off a chunk of his rope and started to twist it and tie it in knots. Normack watched as Ty struggled and worked. As he was finishing, Normack's eyes grew wide and a shiver cascaded down his powerful body. Ty turned to face Normack with something that looked like a horse's bridle in his hands.

"Normack, I know what you're thinking, but I don't have any other ideas. If you bite down on this end, I think I can keep from falling off by holding on to the other end. That is, if you do not mind this in your grip."

Normack looked over at Torg, then back at Ty. "I would kill any other creature that asked that of me. But you are my friend, and I will do this for you with honor."

Ty held out his rope and Normack gently bit down on it just firm enough not to snap it in half.

"Wait, there's one more thing!" Ty realized that if he showed up in town riding on the back of a giant vipercon, it would mean real trouble for him and his family. So he used a strip of black cloth and made a mask to cover his face. This would work really nice to keep his identity a secret.

Ty was ready. He jumped up on Normack's back and held on tight. Then with the determination of a thousand dragons, he called back down to Torg, "I'm sorry, my friend, but there is not enough room up here for the both of us. Try to keep up with us as best as you can."

"What do you mean?" boasted Torg with a sarcastic grin from ear to ear. "It's time you found out what a Zintarian warrior is truly made of. I just hope you two can keep up with me! Now let's make some serious tracks."

Torg flung his bow behind his back and lowered his head. With a flick his tail, he disappeared in a flash.

Ty looked down at Normack and started to laugh. "I didn't think that guy could move that fast. But he had better watch his back because here comes one vipercon on a mission. Okay, Normack, I'm ready, let's finish this!"

Ty held on to that rope for dear life as Normack moved and slid through the forest, like a freight train dancing to music.

"C'mon on, Normack, what are you waiting for? Go faster! You have got to go faster," Ty screamed.

Normack yelled back, "I can't! If I go any faster, you'll die if you fall off."

"If we don't catch up to that thing on time, there'll be nothing left for me to live for. It's all or nothing now. Don't hold back!"

"Then may the winds of luck be with us. Hold on, Ty, hold on tight! Whatever you do, don't let go, or there'll be nothing left of you to bring back to your village."

Ty let out a thunderous roar, ducked down low, and clamped down on those ropes with an iron grip.

Normack took off like a shark in the bloodied water. The wind was whipping through Ty's hair so hard he thought it was going to get ripped right out of his head. The trail looked like a blur; trees and bushes that lined the path looked like a green smudge smeared across the rocky mountainside.

"I still can't see him, Normack. How much farther could he be?"

"I don't know, but his trail is getting fresher, and that can only mean that we must be getting closer."

Determined to get a better look, Ty let go of one hand and stood up on Normack's back. He could hear the chilling sound of trees slamming to the ground by that rinog's rampage echoing through the forest in the distance.

"We are getting closer, Normack. I can hear him," shouted Ty.

"Get down before you kill yourself!" snapped Normack. "We're almost out of the Shadow Forest, just a little farther."

Seconds later, Normack burst out of the forest and into a huge green meadow. Ty almost fell off when he saw the rinog's trail heading straight for his village. He was hoping that Normack was wrong about what he saw, but there was no doubt about it. You could clearly see where the rinog was heading.

"Look over there, Normack. There he is!" yelled Ty. "I can see him. He's headed straight for the razor bushes. Normack, we have to hurry. I doubt if those bushes will stop him. He's crushed everything in his path so far."

That monster was getting closer and closer to the razor bushes, but Normack noticed a small cloud of dust coming up from the trail just up ahead.

Ty started to laugh and said, "Well, would you look at that, Normack? Just over that hill, I think it's Torg. Man, that guy can really move."

"Yes, I see him," said Normack. "And he almost caught up to the rinog."

"Be careful, Torg," screamed Ty. "Don't get too close to those bushes."

However, they were still too far away for Torg to hear them; all they could do was watch.

In just moments, Torg was close enough to make his move. He dove straight at the rinog with his dagger in hand. That rinog must have heard Torg getting closer because as soon as he lunged, the rinog spun around and smashed Torg right in the jaw.

Torg flew twenty-five feet back and landed in a row of tiger cactuses. Their thorns dug in deep, scratching him across his face and down his back. Torg just lay there, as still as a corpse.

"You'll pay dearly for that," yelled Normack. "I promise you. Hey, Torg, we're coming. Just hold on."

The rinog pounded its chest and headed back to where Torg was lying. They watched in horror as it walked over and picked up a boulder and headed back to where Torg was lying. It looked as if it was going to finish him off. You could see the fire in its eyes as it approached him, straining under the boulder's massive weight. Torg had no chance at all; he was at the mercy of that giant, and rinogs never show mercy.

"Don't even think about it," screamed Ty in a voice that exploded across the field like thunder.

The rinog turned around and saw Normack approaching fast, with Ty standing on his back. With a snort, it turned and let out a roar so mighty the grass in the fields lay down as if a wicked wind was sent by the devil himself. It threw that boulder straight at them, but Normack moved just in time as it slammed into the ground, slashing the field open just inches away.

"You're going to have to do better than that, scum bucket," shouted Ty.

It let out another earthshaking roar and headed off toward town. When Normack finally made it to where Torg was lying, the creature was gone.

"Are you all right?" screamed Ty, jumping off Normack's back, prying the bushes free with his bare hands.

Torg slowly opened his eyes and looked around. "Did I get him?"

"Almost," Ty laughed. "If it wasn't for us making so much noise, you would have gotten him."

As soon as Torg sat up, they heard a gruesome sound that I can only describe as sounding like a thousand knives slicing through flesh. They turned and saw the rinog blasting right through the hedge as if it was only a pile of leaves. Nothing was going to stop it now. The ground trembled as it headed straight for Ty's school.

"Are you all right, my friend?" Normack asked.

"Yeah, I'll be alright," Torg mumbled, rubbing his head. "The only thing that hurts is my pride and maybe my jaw a little bit."

"Hey, Torg," said Ty, helping him to his feet, "that was the second time that thing busted you in the chops. If you don't start blocking those hits, he's going to rip your head off."

"Whatever!" said Torg. "I'm just wearing him down!"

Ty stood up and stopped Torg from going any farther. There were so many jagged pieces of razor bushes lying around that if they got any closer, they would be sliced to ribbons.

"Well, what are we waiting for?" shouted Normack. "Jump up and let's get going."

Ty didn't hesitate for a second; he jumped right on Normack's back, then leaned over and helped Torg up. In one swift motion, Normack started to slither over that hedge. You could hear the screeching sounds of the razor bushes scraping and slicing Normack's belly as he slipped past the barricade and into the outskirts of Ty's village.

You could see the path of destruction that led straight for the school. Twisted pieces of bikes and shredded books were scattered everywhere. The swing set Ty loved to play on with his brother was turned into a pile of twisted metal. There wasn't much left of the playground after that rinog ran through it. The sound of kids screaming and crying started to fill the air.

Ty, Normack, and Torg prayed that they weren't too late and nobody was hurt.

"Help those kids," yelled Ty. "Keep them safe inside the school. That's more important than anything. I'm counting on you, Torg."

Torg didn't question him at all. He leaped down and headed straight for the school.

"Don't worry, I will," yelled Torg. "You can count on me."

Just then, three of Ty teachers and came running out from the side of the school, armed with brooms and bats, ready to fight. When they got a look at Ty standing on the back of a vipercon with his armor shining in the bright sunlight, holding his sword up, they stopped dead in their tracks. With their mouths hanging open, they couldn't believe what they saw.

"Get back inside the school and lock the doors," yelled Ty. "My friend Torg will protect you and stand guard."

After they ran back inside, Torg kicked the door closed, then used the bike racks and the chains from the busted-up swing set to barricade the doors tight. In moments, the school was secure. Smiling at a job well-done, he climbed straight up the wall of the school and waved at Ty to tell him that everything was all right.

As soon as Ty got the signal, he looked around to find out where that rinog was now.

"There he goes," shouted Normack. "It's headed right down the street."

"I don't believe it. That's my street over there,'" screamed Ty. "That thing is headed right for my house!"

"He's too far away," shouted Normack. "We'll never catch up to him in time."

"I've got it," Ty screamed. "Normack, quick, grab the top of that tree and pull it down, all the way to the ground. Hurry, you got to do it now."

Normack coiled up, and as fast as lightning, he grabbed the very top of that great tree. Then with all of his might, he started to pull. You could hear that tree pop and creak as Normack used his incredible strength to pull it down. It must have been the hardest thing he had ever done in his life because Normack had to wrap his tail around another tree just to anchor himself down. After two more tugs, that tree's top was lying on the ground by Ty's feet.

"You did it! Thank you, Normack. I'll see you when the battle is over," screamed Ty.

Then he jumped on top of the tree, and with one slice, he chopped the tree loose from Normack's grip.

Ty shot into the air like a bolt of lightning. He was determined that there was nothing in this world that would stand in his way. Ty was no longer afraid of anything. He finally realized that he had always had the power to do what he knew was right, and nothing could ever take that from him. He remembered how scared he was the first time he saw a rinog, but all he felt now was that he couldn't wait until he had his hands around its throat. It was time to make things right again, and that rinog wasn't going to stop him.

CHAPTER 12

The Battle Of All Battles

Ty could see the people below in shock as they stared up at the sky, watching as he flew over their heads. All the men in town came running out of their homes after the rinog, armed with anything they could grab, but Ty knew they wouldn't stand a chance. It would be up to him.

"Stay inside!" Ty shouted, zipping over the trees. "Keep your families safe. This is my fight. I will deal with that rinog myself."

As Ty flew closer, he saw the beast crossing the street in front of his house, heading right for his yard. The sound of popping and cracking burst up from below as his favorite climbing tree in his neighbor's yard slammed to the ground.

Ty grit his teeth, and with a thunderous voice, he roared out, "You've caused enough trouble around here and now I'm mad! I know a cool game. Wanna play?"

The rinog turned around, looked up at Ty, and let out a bone-chilling grunt as smoke shot out from its nostrils.

Ty held his shield tightly against his shoulder and tightened up every muscle in his body. "Tag, you're it!" Ty shouted out with the roar of a titan.

There was absolutely nothing that rinog could do except watch as Ty attacked with the fury of a thunderstorm, slamming into that monster with all his might.

Kaboooom! The shock wave of that mighty blow echoed across the land like thunder. He hit him so hard that the windows in his neighbor's house shattered from that deafening blast and sent the rinog flipping across the street and crashing into old man Grady's pool.

Ty slowly stood up, shaking his head, trying to regain his strength after that incredible impact. "Where do you think you're going?" asked Ty. "You started this fight, and it's about time I finished it."

Ty raced across the street, heading straight for old man Grady's backyard. He jumped over the tree and darted around the back of the house just in time to see that rinog lying facedown in sand and muck. The pool was totally destroyed. Shards of twisted pieces of steel were scattered all across the yard while chunks of its blue liner went floating away in a river of water down the street.

"Looks like that bath didn't cool your temper down at all," Ty shouted.

Watching closely as it slowly crawled to its feet, Ty braced himself for whatever that creature had in mind. It just stood there wobbly and dazed, like a statue carved out of stone. With its huge muscles rippling in the soft sunlight, it lowered its head, gazing at Ty with burning hatred. The dripping wet satchel, full of blue fire rubies, was still clenched tightly in its grip. There was no doubt about it. That rinog wanted to rip Ty's heart right out of his chest.

Oh yeah! It was on.

Ty stood there, bravely and confidently staring straight into the face of the gigantic rinog. This monster must be at least ten feet tall. Its eyes glowed with anger, and every muscle in its body throbbed with hatred. Ty wasn't afraid at all; he just stood there defiantly with his shield held high and his sword held tightly by his side.

Suddenly, old man Grady kicked his back door open with a kitchen knife in one hand and a fork in the other. "Look what you've done to my pool, you … you … you, what the heck are you?"

"Get back inside and lock your doors," replied Ty. "He's mine!"

Then Ty jumped onto that smashed tree stump and roared like a lion in the forest, "You better drop my bag of blue fire rubies, horn

DAVID WALKER

head, and leave this place forever, or I swear to you that I will kick your butt all the way back to the Shadow Forest."

With that, the rinog let out a growl that would have sent shivers down the spine of the devil himself.

"So what are you waiting for, you bag of worms? Are you afraid of a fair fight?" exclaimed Ty once again.

Now that was all that the rinog could take; it started to charge. The ground trembled as it ripped through the yard toward Ty, sending grass and mud flying in the air. You could see some of Ty's neighbors peeking out of their hiding places, watching in shock and horror while Jace and Carson, two of the high school football players, snuck back and forth cautiously behind the trees, looking for an opportunity to attack. But Ty just stood his ground—strong, defiant, and alone. It was too late to reconsider his plans or wait for Normack and Torg.

Ty patiently waited as it got closer and closer. It was as if nothing else existed; there were no sounds of bird in the trees or even the faint sounds of children. The town was so still that even the soft warm breeze faded to nothing. All you could hear was the sound of the rinog's pounding steps on the cold, hard ground.

With a hideous crash, they met in battle. Ty hit that rinog with all his strength, matching it blow for blow. His shield was blackened with dirt and mud as they rolled across the ground, pounding each other with everything they had. Then with a surprising move, Ty jumped on its back and wrapped his arms around the rinog's neck. It thrashed all around, struggling wildly, trying to knock Ty off, but he held on tight. After a few seconds, it realized that it couldn't shake Ty loose, so it looked for the biggest tree around and slammed into it so hard that it ripped right out of the ground and burst its trunk into splinters. But Ty saw what it was planning to do, and in a split second before that mighty impact, he let go and tumbled into a deep ditch.

"Missed me, horn head?" he called out.

The rinog turned around, then tore off a huge branch with a loud grunt and dove into that ditch, swinging wildly.

Clouds of dirt and grass shot out in every direction as it tried to pulverize Ty with that chunk of timber. But Ty was way too fast for him and hacked his way through that savage attack with his sword.

"It's not going to be that easy," shouted Ty. "You have no idea who you're messing with!"

In a flash, Ty jumped out of the ditch and spun around, smashing that beast with his sword in the back of its head, knocking the rinog face-first into the mud again. A blow like that would take the head off any other creature, but the rinog just shook it off. Ty knew he had to get that beast away from the middle of town, so he figured he should lure it to the river's edge. That way, no innocent people would get hurt and he could finish the fight there.

As soon as that rinog stood up, Ty jumped up and came crashing down on its head with a powerful blow again. *Crack!* This time, he hit it with his shield so hard that it sent shock waves rippling across the ground.

"How did that feel?" shouted Ty. "Because if you want some more, you'll have to catch me."

Ty took off as fast as he could across old man Grady's backyard and down the street. Then as soon as he passed the old willow tree, he headed down the hidden trail he always took with his friends.

The rinog charged at Ty as fast as a six-legged fire rasp and catching up quick. Fortunately, Ty knew that trail like the back of his hand; he knew where all the soft sandy ground was, and he led it straight into a murky sinkhole.

With a huge crunch, it fell face-first into the biggest sinkhole in town. Chest deep, roaring with a thunderous vengeance, it thrashed wildly to get out of the deep pit, but it never let go of Ty's sack of blue fire rubies. All Ty could do was stand there and watch as it slowly made its way to the edge of the pit and climb back out. Frustrated that his trick didn't work, Ty took off for the river's edge once again.

The rinog was so blinded by the desire to kill Ty that it got down on all four legs and charged with a monstrous fury.

Ty made it to the edge of the river just a few steps ahead of the charging monster. With a quick move, he jumped onto a log, flipped over the rinog, and landed a tremendous blow with his sword across its back. *Smack!*

"I'm right behind you, horn head," yelled Ty. "So drop the sack and leave this place before you get hurt."

The beast didn't listen to a word Ty was saying. Its heart was full of hatred, and its eyes were blinded with rage. It continued its attack with a fury never seen before. It swung wildly as it tried to beat, smash, or crush Ty to death.

Ty jumped back into the water to avoid the rinog's savage attacks. Hit after hit, they tumbled and wrestled across the shore. The river seemed to explode with rage as the fight ripped through its waters. Ty hit the monster with all his might, trying as hard as he could to stop it, but the more they fought, the harder it attacked. Ty knew he couldn't take much more of this and decided he had to end it fast before the monster killed him. He knew that his only chance to defeat it was to use all his skills and outwit it.

In a flash, he got an idea and turned back toward town, running straight for the great pit. But the rinog was standing a bit too close, and its reflexes were as sharp as a razor. Just like that, it reached down and snatched Ty off his feet. It finally had him right where it wanted him. Ty tried as hard as he could, but the rinog had him locked solidly around his waist with a crushing grip. The more Ty struggled, the tighter it squeezed. Ty looked all around, but Normack and Torg were nowhere around. He was all alone in its cold grip of death.

Ty started to get angrier and angrier. You could see the emotion starting to boil deep inside him like a blazing volcano, red with power and boiling with passion. There was no more fear left in his eyes or panic in his heart. Ty was a warrior with the heart of a black dragon.

It was an amazing thing to watch as Ty's eyes started to turn red with the power of justice and the mighty strength of determination. The rinog kept squeezing as hard as he could, but Ty's armor held strong. That beast thought that it had Ty where it wanted him, but it was Ty that had the rinog just where he needed him.

Ty reached out with the strength of ten men and grabbed ahold of the rinog's horn with his left hand, then pulled it right up to his face and stared right into its glowing eyes. Its breath was burning hot and smelled like the sulfur that burned in the deepest pits of demon's cave.

Then with a voice that shook the graves of his ancestors, Ty yelled out, "You have terrorized the people of Zintar, you have caused great devastation to the people and creatures of this valley, and you have stolen treasures from me. You are to drop that sack and leave here forever, or you will die here today!"

The rinog let out a mighty roar and started smashing down on Ty's head with all its strength. But Ty blocked every explosive punch with his shield, sending a shower of sparks flying in all directions.

Ty shook that great beast's head and then pulled it closely again. "Stop this now," shouted Ty, "or you will leave me no choice!"

That is when the rinog spoke out for the first time in a voice that sounded like an earthquake ripping through the walls of the earth. "Who do you think you are to order me to do anything? I will crush your bones into dust and take whatever I want, whenever I want, and you cannot stop me."

Ty looked deep into its eyes and said boldly, "I am Cobasfang from the Shadow Forest and you will obey me, or you will regret being born!"

"You're Cobasfang?" it laughed wildly. "Not only will I kill you, but when I am done with you, I am also going to kill everyone that lives in this place just for fun."

Ty held his head up high and roared out like thunder, "I am Cobasfang from the Shadow Forest. I banish you from these meadows forever, and you will never trespass into the caves of the lost souls again." Then Ty held his sword high into the air, and as the light sparkled off its razor edge, he shouted, "You are banished!"

Then Ty slammed the hilt of his sword deep into the rinog's arm. It ripped right through its tough hide like butter and dug deep into its flesh. Its eyes opened wide with pain as it let out an earth-shattering howl that echoed across the land.

The rinog threw Ty and the sack of rubies across the beach and grabbed its arm with a blood-curdling scream, then fell to the ground, kicking and rolling in pain.

There must have been some venom left in Normack's fang that Ty had used for the hilt of his sword because the rinog's arm started to curl and twist, then turn black as coal.

Ty hopped up on that tree stump and shouted, "Leave now and never return. I am protecting this land. If you ever return to this place again, I will not show you mercy. You will be destroyed!"

With that, the rinog turned and ran across the river, disappearing into the thick forest. Ty was still a bit dizzy and hurting from head to toe, so he sat back down in his favorite spot next to the great pit to rest for a minute.

Suddenly, he heard the sound of soft footsteps approaching. When he turned around, he got the surprise of his life. It was his little brother, Bob. He was so excited to see his brother he nearly jumped in the air, but he knew he couldn't let him find out who he was. So he disguised his voice the best he could.

"Are you okay, mister?" Bob asked.

"I sure am," replied Ty. "I am Cobasfang. I have a gift for your grandmother and all that live here in this village. You don't have to worry about that rinog ever coming back here again. Now take this sack of blue fire rubies to your mom. She will know what to do." Ty tossed the rubies into Bob's red wagon and smiled.

"Wait, there's one more thing." Ty drew his sword and cut the string to his pouch that was filled with jewels from around his waist. "Give this to your father. It is a gift from your brother, Ty. Tell him not to worry. Ty will be home soon, and he told me to tell you that he loves you."

Bob was so excited that he started running back home.

"Wait, you forgot your wagon," Ty chuckled.

"Oh yeah, sorry," Bob replied as he stopped and looked back.

Ty got in the back of the wagon and helped push it through the dirt until he made it to the street. Then waving goodbye, he stood there smiling as his brother headed home. The wheels of his wagon were squeaking and wobbling as he turned the corner next to his uncle John's ice-cream store.

Ty sat down again with a smile on his face, then stabbed the ground with his sword and leaned on its bloody hilt. As he started to regain his strength, Normack and Torg came strolling over the hill and sat down next to him.

"It's good to see you again," said Normack. "Are you all right?"

"Yeah, I'll be okay. I don't think that rinog will ever bother this place or Zintar again."

Torg sat down next to Ty and gave him a nudge. "I saw that you gave the sack of blue fire rubies to that little boy a moment ago. Who was that?"

Ty just smiled. "That boy was my brother, and everything is going to be fine now. Except there's one little thing I've got to get back to."

"What's that?" asked Torg.

"My ring that Queen Lylah gave me must have fallen into the great pit, and I want it back!"

Normack leaned down and let out a sigh. "Looks to me like you cannot hold on to your things very well. The last time you lost something, it nearly killed us all. Is that ring worth your life? That place stinks of cave rats. Don't you remember the last time you tangled with one?"

"I remember. You don't have to worry about me anymore. I mean, how much trouble can we possibly get into?"

Then he pulled his star crystal from his pocket and turned to Torg. "Would you do me a favor and tie this off somewhere real tight?" Then tossed Torg the end of his rope and dove headfirst down into the pit.

Torg couldn't believe what Ty just did, but he moved like lightning and tied the end around a big tree stump next to the pit.

"What in the world does that guy think he is doing, Normack?"

"Getting his ring back, I guess," laughed Normack as he went down the hole after him.

"You two guys are nuts," shouted Torg as he headed down the slippery walls of that great pit too.

CHAPTER 13

A Dark Beginning

The great pit was believed to be a dangerous place indeed, filled with mystery and dark vicious creatures. Nobody had ever ventured to go down there before. That is, not until Ty dove in!

Ty sailed down into that pit like a rocket with Normack and Torg streaking right behind him. You could hear their voices echoing off the walls of the pit as they yelled and shouted with fearful excitement.

"Slow down," yelled Normack. "You're going too fast. That ring isn't going anywhere, and this is not a race."

"Sure it is! The faster we get to the bottom, the quicker I'll get my ring back!" Ty yelled back.

As they traveled deeper and deeper, Ty's eyes sprung open wide as he let out a thunderous scream, "Oh no!" But it was too late. *Crack!* Ty reached the end of his rope and spun out of control like a top on the end of a string.

"Hold on, Ty! We're right behind you," hissed Normack as loud as he could.

"Oh, man, I'm getting dizzy! Yahoo," Ty hollered. "Hey, Torg, it looks like the express ride from here on out."

"What do you mean?" Torg screeched in panic. "What are you doing? Hey, stop that! Are you nuts? You're going to kill yourself!"

Ty didn't care at all; he just held his star crystal over his head, then cut the end of the rope with his sword. "Last one down is a rotten egg," echoed off the slimy walls as Ty disappeared into the darkness.

"Catch him, Normack, before he kills himself."

But Ty was too far ahead of them when he sliced that rope. In seconds, Ty was able to start making out the faint shadows of the bottom of the pit getting closer. In a flashback, Ty remembered the last time he fell down a deep hole, and he wasn't going to hit bottom like that again. So just as he was going to splatter on the ground below, he pulled out his knife and stabbed it deep into the heart of the great pit's wall. Then holding on as tight as he could, he started slicing a long gash into its side. The sound of stone grinding on stone rippled down the cavern as he slowed himself down just enough to make it to the bottom safely.

"Nice move!" shouted Normack. "But if you try a stunt like that again, I'll kill you myself!"

"This is nasty! Hey, Torg, I thought this place would be like all the other places we've been in. But this place is covered in trash. It's like people were throwing their filthy garbage down this pit for years. It's going to be imposable to find my ring in all this crud!"

"Don't worry, we'll help you no matter how long it takes."

As soon as Normack and Torg landed in that heap of trash, they started to rummage around in the nasty pile of junk. There were old bottles, rotting chunks of food, and old rusty cans scattered everywhere. There was even an old rusty bike with little flower stickers on the handle bars smashed against the rocks.

The more they searched, the more impossible it seemed that they would ever find that ring. But Ty wasn't about to give up so quickly. He tore into that mess and searched as hard as he could.

Finally, after hours of digging and scooping through clumps of nasty crud, Torg popped up out of a small pile of clothes and started jumping up and down like a little kid. "I got it, I got it. Hey, Ty, who's the man? C'mon, say it. Who's the man?"

"Did you really find it? Dude, you're the man!" Ty was so excited that he almost fell on his face as he made his way over to Torg. But as soon as he got close enough to see Torg's face, Ty busted out laughing.

You see, while Torg was jumping around holding Ty's ring up in the air, he never noticed that he was covered from head to toe with old women's clothes. He had a yellow dress wrapped around his waist and a pink scarf hanging over his shoulder. Ty and Normack started rolling with laughter.

While Torg struggled to unwrap the scarf from around his neck, Ty and Normack suddenly stopped laughing and their smiles quickly disappeared. The look on Ty's face began to fill with anger as he watched Torg throw the rag to the ground. Before Normack could make a sound, Ty reached down, grabbed his knife, and threw it right at Torg's head. His knife whizzed through the air and missed Torg's head by a whisper as he dove out of the way.

"Are you crazy?" shouted Torg.

The chilling sound of a solid thud echoed across the cave floor as Ty's knife stuck right into the chest of a huge cave rat lurking in the shadows. Then smooth as silk, Ty grabbed his bow and sent two arrows whistling across the cave and into that filthy rat just as it lunged to attack.

An eerie squeal ricocheted down the cold black tunnels as the cave rat fell by Torg's feet. Twitching and snapping its yellow sharp teeth, it lunged one last time at Torg's throat. This time, Torg was ready; he swung around and kicked it as hard as he could, sending it crashing onto that small bike in the corner. As its tail slowly thumped to the ground, Torg turned and muttered back to them, "I think we're in serious trouble."

Normack rushed over and stood tall above it, his fangs glistening in the light of Ty's star crystal. "I told you it was too dangerous down here. This place is covered with trash and a perfect feeding ground. There must be thousands of these beasts everywhere."

"I know. I know you did. But we're here now, and there's nothing I can do about it. Look, guys, the walls of that pit is way too muddy to climb up. We've got no other choice but to head deeper underground and go through these rat tunnels. I'm sure one of them will lead to back to the surface!"

Normack looked over at Ty and flicked his tongue. "You sure do know how to get into trouble, don't you? Except for this time, we're all trapped in a twisted maze of tunnels that are infested with deadly cave rats."

Ty just smiled and chuckled a little bit. "What are you worried about, Normack? We're going to be just fine. I've got the perfect plan. I think we should head into the cave over there next to Torg because it looks big enough for your big fat head to fit through, and it looks like it might lead back into the Shadow Forest. You know, Normack, while you were taking a nap, Torg and I ran into a few of these cave rats in the tunnels by the crystal mountain. So if we're lucky, we might be able to make our way back there and get out."

Torg shook his head in disbelief. "You must be crazy! If we head back in that direction, we are going to end up back at the caves of the lost souls. Don't you remember what happened back there? What do you think is going to happen if we run into another Norgon hunting party? I don't think we'll be able to hide with a fifty-foot vipercon by our side! I think that rinog hit you in the head too hard."

By the look on Normack's face, you could tell he had no idea what Torg was talking about. So Torg filled him in on the dangers that lay ahead if they should meet up with a pack of Norgon warriors.

Normack was obviously upset; he was gritting his teeth and flicking his tail sharply back and forth. "Tell me, Ty. Is that little ring of yours worth the danger you put us all in?"

Ty got so upset that he picked up a stone and shattered it against the wall, then walked right up to Normack and got in his face. "I didn't ask you to follow me down here, and I never meant to put you in any danger. I know that I can't climb back up that slippery pit wall, but I'm sure that you and Torg can. So you guys can take off right now if you want!"

Normack shook his head and then took a deep breath to calm down. "We're not going to leave you down here on your own, you fish feet! All we're saying is that you have to start thinking things through. Did it even cross your mind that diving headfirst into this pit might not be such a bright idea? Or how about challenging Grog to a fistfight? And oh yeah, let's not forget that bright idea of yours to fight a rinog all by yourself. Don't you see? You have to start making better decisions before it gets you killed. We're a team and we're going with you, but you got to start using that head of yours."

Ty walked over to the dead rat, stepped on its head, and pried his knife and arrows free. "You're right, Normack. I'm sorry I wasn't thinking. I just wanted to get my ring back. I guess I have a lot to learn about this Cobasfang stuff. Thanks for sticking with me."

Now all three of them understood the dangers that could be lurking in the shadows ahead, but they made up their minds that they were going to face them together. Normack, Ty, and Torg had proven themselves to be strong and valiant warriors, but the treacherous journey that awaited them would put their friendship and stamina to the ultimate test.

Just as they started to head down that cold and dark tunnel, they heard a strange slithering sound from behind. As they spun around, Torg spotted Ty's rope landing on the pile of trash.

"All right, I wanted my rope back! Someone up there must have seen it tied to that old tree stump and tossed it down the hole! You see, guys, somebody up there is looking out for us. We'll be fine."

CHAPTER 14

The Forbidden Land

Ty, Torg, and Normack all took a deep breath and then started on their journey to find their way out. That long, deep pit sent them into the heart of the underworld. To make matters worse, the cave they chose was cold and damp, and the walls seemed alive with thousands of huge roaches scurrying up and down.

"This place gives me the creeps," Ty mumbled at Torg. "Have you ever seen so many dead roaches all over the walls and the ground like this before?"

"That's not dead roaches we're walking on, Ty. This whole place is littered with splintered pieces of bones and chewed up skulls. That's the crunching sound you're hearing when we walk."

"Holy crap! You're right. Now I'm totally creeped out!"

Torg nodded (as if to say he was too), then with a reassuring smile, he turned and took the lead, descending through the cave. Ty and Normack stayed back and watched silently as Torg cautiously cleared the way. His tail flicked nervously back and forth as he headed out of sight.

But he didn't make it very far at all before he stopped, turned around, and waved to Normack. "Pssst, Normack, come over here. Can you smell that? I don't like this. I don't like this at all. I can smell the moldy nests of a hundred cave rats. We must be getting close to their lair!"

Normack made his way to where Torg was crouched down, then flicked his tongue and thought for a moment. "You're right. I can taste their young in the air. The scent is coming from these cracks in the wall. There must be another cave right next to us. Be on the lookout for any small openings that they can fit through."

"I will. Just be ready to get out fast if we're spotted."

"Torg, be careful. We'll be right behind you."

Ty was getting nervous as he listened to their soft whispers drifting through the cave. So as soon as Torg turned and started to leave, he ran up to Normack and tapped him on his back. "I heard what you said. How big of an opening should we be looking out for?"

"Any opening large enough for them to fit their heads through. If their heads can fit, then they can squeeze through. So watch out for any opening that's small enough for *you* to squeeze through, but don't forget, their young can be just as dangerous when they attack as a pack. They can fit through an opening as small as your fist."

"Great, you mean they can come out from anywhere?"

"Yeah, now you got it."

Torg's tail slapped the ground with a pop as he turned quickly and stared at Normack. "Shhhh. Would you two be quiet? They don't need any help from you two. It's bad enough they can probably smell us, but those things have sharp hearing too!"

Normack and Ty just looked at each other and didn't say another word as they followed Torg deeper into the tunnel. The sounds of rats scurrying back and forth behind the walls started to get louder. Chills ran down their spines as they crept through the darkness. No matter how hard they tried, the crackling sounds of each step they took seemed to call out to every cave rat for a mile. Here comes lunch.

Torg took his time and scouted out the area ahead, making sure to point out every hidden entrance the rats could use to ambush them. Each time he passed a large opening, he looked around for anything he could use to seal it up. With rocks and chunks of roots, he silently jammed them into the openings. He knew it wouldn't last long, but it might give them enough time to escape if they tried to come through.

As they sneaked through the tunnel and deeper into the earth, the floor became less covered with bones and the stench of the cave rat nests started to fade away.

"We must be getting out of their hunting grounds," whispered Torg. "The air is getting fresher, and the ground is becoming cool and dry again."

Normack made his way back to Torg and flicked his tongue a few more times. "I think you're right. I don't see any sign of them now. But I don't get it. Why wouldn't they come down here?"

"I don't know. This place is perfect for cave rats. It doesn't make any sense. Now where's Ty?"

As they turned around, they saw him gazing at the wall with his hands on his hips and looking puzzled. "Hey, Torg, what is this stuff on the walls over here? It looks like someone smeared wiggling green lightning bug guts all over it."

Torg stopped and walked back to where he was and looked very closely. "I don't know what that stuff is. I've never seen anything like it before. Just stay away from it. It could be poisonous! C'mon, let's go."

Torg turned and headed back to where Normack was.

"Hey, Torg, at least it doesn't stink like Normack's breath. This stuff smells good. It almost smells like honey."

"I said leave it alone!" snapped Torg. "Now c'mon, I said let's go!"

However, Ty just couldn't leave well enough alone. He wanted to check it out so badly that he grabbed his knife and started chipping away at a root that was covering over a long slender strip. But as soon as he started to slice into that slime, it started to wiggle around, then it sucked back inside the wall in a flash.

"Did you see that? That stuff zipped under these rocks like it was alive!"

As Normack and Torg turned to see what Ty was talking about, the ground started to rumble and shake.

"What in the world did you do now!" shouted Normack. "What part of leave it alone didn't you understand?"

"It wasn't me. I didn't do anything!"

The glowing green slime on the walls started to boil and erupt in a blistering frenzy. Everybody dove for the ground as pieces of thick chunks of slime spewed out from every crack.

"We got to get out of here right now!" shouted Normack. "Follow me, you two. There's a cavern up ahead!" Normack didn't waste a second as he spun around and slithered as fast as he could across the ground like a wave.

Ty glanced over at Normack and nodded. "We're right behind you. C'mon, Torg, this stuff's like glue. Hurry up and grab my hand!"

Just as Torg reached up to grab Ty's hand, a sharp blast exploded right behind them, sending a large chunk of the wall smashing into Ty's back. He went flipping across the cave, headfirst into a crystal pillar next to a large puddle of goop.

Torg watched in shock as Ty's body slammed into that pillar and collapsed to the ground like a dead rat. "I'm coming, Ty!" screamed Torg as he sprung up and headed for him. Trying desperately to avoid the puddles of slime boiling up from the ground, Torg took to the air and clawed his way straight up the steep walls, then pounced between the sharp and jagged pillars as the sludge slowly covered the cave floor.

"Stop playing around!" Normack shouted as a bubbling wave swept away Torg's only safe spot to land.

"I don't think so!" boasted Torg as he pried a large crystal free from the side of the wall and sent it slamming into the ground just inches from Ty. The horrendous thud echoed like thunder as the wave splashed against its side.

"I've got you now!" hollered Torg as he sprung down from the side of that cave, flakes of stone dust smoked off his claws as he sailed through the damp air.

With the grace of a spirit cat, Torg landed on that pillar and dug his claws in deep. "It's time to go, my friend" whispered Torg as he gently rolled Ty over and sat him against the pillar. "Ty, are you all right?"

Ty slowly opened his eyes up and held his head as he spit some blood on the ground. "Yeah, that thing hits like a rinog!"

"Let's get out of here!" Torg shouted as he helped him to his feet. "This place is caving in!"

"Okay, Bob, lets go home. Dylan said we're going fishing after dinner, and I've got some homework to do," muttered Ty in a daze as he staggered to his feet.

"What did you say?"

Ty turned toward Torg with a grin on his face as his knees started to buckle. He collapsed to the ground.

"Normack, Ty's hurt! I'll get you out of here, buddy. Just hang on." Torg reached down and snatched him off the ground, then slung him over his shoulder like a cold sack of dirt and bolted for the exit.

Torg ran as fast as he could as the rocky ground started to split and crumble.

"Run faster! Move those feet of yours!" shouted Normack as loud as he could.

Torg desperately scratched his way over the last clumps of rocks to stay out of that green slime as it bubbled up from the splintered floor.

"C'mon, you can make it. Just a little farther!"

"I'm coming as fast as I can, you bigmouthed legless lizard!"

Torg ran as hard he could, but the air became thick and hard to breathe as that sweet overpowering smell filled the cavern. Torg was getting dizzy, weaker, his lungs were collapsing. That sweet smell was a poisonous gas, and he was passing out.

Normack swayed back and forth nervously as he watched Torg start to stumble and struggle as he carried Ty. Normack couldn't wait any longer and bolted out of the safety of that cavern, heading straight for them. By the time he got there, the bubbling slime had already surrounded them and it was quickly closing in. Normack watched in horror as Torg staggered one last time and started to fall into the slime.

With a thunderous growl, Normack rose up and grabbed Torg and Ty around their waist. Trying with all his might to keep his fangs from slicing through their tender bodies, he bit down as hard as he could, then with all the strength he had left, Normack picked them up and bolted toward the cavern. He stretched across the jagged rocks and razor-sharp crystals as the cave quickly filled up beneath him. He knew he had to move fast if he was to make his way safely to the cavern up ahead. With a sudden desperate lunge, Normack shot across the top of a boulder as it fell into the muck, blocking the flow of slime as he landed safely into the cavern.

Normack spun around and coiled up as he set them down as gently as he could, far away from the fumes of that bubbling death trap. "Wake up, you two. Take a deep breath of this fresh air!"

Ty slowly opened his eyes and started coughing and gagging up what was left of the poisonous fumes. "What in the world was that stuff?"

"I don't know. But if it wasn't for Torg, you would've never made it out of there alive!"

Ty sat there for a moment, trying to make sense of what just happened, then turned around and saw Torg lying on the ground next to him. After a few moments, his head started to clear and he reached back and gave Torg a gentle nudge across his shoulders.

"Hey, buddy, are you all right? Wake up. You're safe now."

Torg rolled his head around and looked over at Ty and started to cough up the poisonous gas. He lay there on his side, hacking and spitting out green chunks as he struggled to breathe again.

"No wonder there were no cave rats around, Normack," coughed Torg. "That place was a living death trap!"

Normack looked around and shook his head. "There's one more thing we have to consider. With all that shouting and all that noise, every creature down here knows exactly where we are. So I guess we don't have to whisper anymore."

"Now that's the spirit!" laughed Ty. "I never did like sneaking around anyway. I would rather walk down these caverns and make those creatures hide from us than us hiding from them!"

Normack lowered his head and went right up to Ty. "I would like to agree with you, but whoever said cave rats would ever hide from anything?"

"Look, you two, cave rats aren't the only thing we have to worry about," mumbled Torg. "Don't forget where we are. We have to keep a sharp eye out for Norgons too. We were lucky to make it out alive the last time we ran into a pack of those demons, and now our only escape route is blocked by that goop over there. We had better play it smart if we are going to make it out of this one alive!"

Ty and Normack knew that he was right, and after all that commotion, they knew that if there were any Norgons around, they had to get out of there fast before they had company.

Ty reached over and helped Torg to his feet. "You're right again. We better get out of here fast. How do you feel? Can you make it?"

"No problem, and I've got a pretty good idea which way to go. I'll take the lead, and if I come up to a split in the cave, I'll mark which way I went by scratching an arrow on the ceiling with my sword. No one will ever think of looking up there for my trail, so just remember to check the roof if we get separated."

"That's a real sneaky trick, Torg. Did Scales teach you that one?" chuckled Ty.

"No, that one I taught him," snickered Torg as he slapped Ty on his back.

Now Normack reluctantly shook his head and agreed to the plan, then watched in silence as Torg walked off into the darkness.

"You're next, Normack."

"All right. Now remember, don't follow too closely. If we run into trouble, we'll need you to make sure nothing sneaks up from behind!"

Then with a strong whip of his tail, Normack took off, skimming across the jagged rocks and disappearing in the blink of an eye.

Ty waited for a moment like Normack said, then picked up his star crystal and took a deep breath. He had a pounding headache from the terrible crash against that pillar, and his heart was beating with fear and excitement as he stood there staring into the blackness. "Well, I guess it's my turn," he murmured to himself as he turned and started down that cave behind his friends.

Ty walked cautiously at first, listening for any sign of danger. The gentle footsteps of Torg and Normack's swooshing slither slowly disappeared behind the gentle sounds of water dripping in a haunting rhythm, filling the shallow murky puddles.

Where in the world are those two? Ty quietly thought to himself. This cave seemed to go on for miles, and the deeper he went, the harder the ground started to become. Torg's and Normack's tracks slowly disappeared. He felt alone again; his body was aching and his fingers were getting numb from the cold damp air. Ty tried his best to keep his spirits up, but after he walked for about an hour, he came upon a large gash in the side of that cave that branched off into three directions.

As he looked around, he could not find a single track anywhere. There were no marks on the ceiling or carvings on the wall. He wasn't sure what direction they went. Ty held his star crystal as high as he could, pacing back and forth between each opening.

"Torg, Normack, where are you guys?" Ty whispered as loudly as he could. "C'mon, Torg, Normack, which way do I go?"

But there was no answer at all. So he studied each opening as hard as he could, looking for the smallest sign that could help him find his friends. The more he looked, the more frustrated he became. Ty had to make a decision. He figured that he should try the widest path because Normack might not be able to fit through the other two if the walls started to close in.

Ty was mad and frustrated at himself that he had lost the trail of his friends, but he wasn't going to let that slow him down. So he drew his sword and slashed an arrow deep into the stone above. With no other choice and determined to find his friends, Ty boldly headed into that cave alone.

As he got farther into the depths of that cave, the walls seemed to get warmer, and he started to see small spiders and lizards scurrying around on the floor. Ty started to smile a little bit because he knew that if there were spiders around, then there must be food around for them. There had to be an opening around here somewhere to the outside world. In fact, Ty got so excited he started walking even faster, looking all over for more clues to where an exit might be.

The air began to become fresher and cleaner. "I must be getting close," Ty muttered to himself. Soon, he started to feel a gentle, warm breeze. "There it is! I found a way out!" shouted Ty as he looked behind a stone wedged against the wall. The glistening sunlight was a welcome sight indeed. Ty pulled out his sword, pried the stone loose, and laughed out loud as it slammed to the ground with a loud crash.

As Ty looked around, he knew right away that Torg and Normack didn't come this way because there were no tracks in the powdery dust on the floor. So he ran back as fast as he could to meet up with them so they could all get out of this place together.

Ty ran all the way back through the cave, jumping and hurtling over the boulders he had to sneak over just moments ago. When he got back to the cavern, he slid to a stop, then yelled out as loudly as he could. "Hey, you two, where are you guys? I found a way out of here!"

But there was no answer. His words just echoed into the darkness. So he took out his sword and sliced an *X* on the side of that cave to mark the way out. Then with excitement in his heart, Ty ran down the next opening after his friends. It only took a few minutes until he spotted Normack's smooth trail brushed against some moss on the floor.

"Normack, Torg, where are you guys?" he cautiously whispered. But again, his voice disappeared into the silence.

Ty started to get that uneasy feeling of danger lurking close by again, so he slowly drew his sword and raised his star crystal a little bit higher to get a better look at what was surrounding him. The only sound left in the cave was the sound of his heart beating softly in his chest.

After a deep breath, he slowly and silently crept deeper into the cavern until he spotted two huge boulders sprawled across the floor. They were hiding the entrance to an even larger cave below. So he ducked down, slid his star crystal back into his pouch, and crawled on his belly over to the boulders ahead.

Slowly, he peeked around the edge of the cold stone wall, only to see the broken remains of what must have been a great battle. Once Ty saw Torg's knife lying on the ground, covered with green blood still fresh on its blade, it only took a second to figure out what had happened.

CHAPTER 15

Against All Odds

A stone-cold silence fell over Ty like the bitter wet blanket of a winter's rainstorm. There were shards of arrows and busted chunks of twisted chain scattered across the ground. Ty climbed down the jagged cliff's wall and crept through the cavern, studying every mark and footprint on the ground. He found huge gouges gashed into the thick stone walls where axes hacked deep. There was a mighty battle here indeed, and by the marks left on the ground, he knew that his friends were captured by at least twenty Norgon warriors.

Ty dropped his sword and fell to the ground in shock. He tried to hold back his tears as he looked around. He knew that they never should have separated. They should have just stayed together because when they were together, they were invincible.

With tears in his eyes, he picked up Torg's knife that was lying in the slimy muck, wiped it off clean, and then tucked it in his boot.

There was a fire in his eyes that burned bright with anger as he stared down the lonely cave ahead. Those Norgon scums were going to be in the fight of their lives!

He started to take off, running down the trail left by the Norgons, then stopped dead in his tracks. He suddenly realized that, if he wasn't careful, he would get himself captured too. So he thought for a moment, then climbed back up the side of that steep and treacherous cliff wall and made his way down a narrow ledge, hiding in the cold dark shadows and lurking behind rocks. He had to be careful not to be seen or heard if he had any chance to rescue his friends. That is, if they were still alive and those monsters haven't had them for lunch yet.

The farther he traveled, the more he started to hear the faint sounds of clanging armor and pounding footsteps began to drift through the air from the cavern below. The tracks he was following led him right into an underground Norgon fortress. Carved out of solid stone, its lifeless ground was littered with the bones of a thousand beasts. Ty crawled closer and closer until the choking black smoke from the torches on the walls below made his eyes burn and sting.

Ty sat back for a moment and wondered what to do next. He turned around and peered down again and watched in fear as a troop of warriors marched into the iron gates. It was a struggle for him to stay any longer in that thick smoke, so he used a rag to cover his mouth to keep from gagging on the smoke and stench from rotting flesh that swirled around the high cavern walls.

"There's no way I'll ever sneak in there without being seen," he mumbled to himself. Then as the fear started to slowly slip away, his heart became full of courage as his body tensed with rage.

I don't know what crazy idea went through Ty's head, but he stood up from behind the thick black boulder he was hiding behind. Then with a powerful leap, he jumped all the way down and landed solidly in front of the rusty iron gates of the Norgons' city!

With his shield by his side and his sword held high, Ty shouted out in a voice that sounded like the crack of thunder during a midnight storm, "I am Cobasfang! Lord of all in the Shadow Forest. You have two of my friends, and I command you to release them now!"

The tower guards didn't know what to do. They began running back and forth, grabbing their weapons and slamming the doors behind them. Ty didn't have to wait long for his answer as a cloud of arrows filled the air, screaming a song of death as they headed straight for him!

Ty raised his shield, knelt on one knee, and braced himself as the horde of poison arrows and twisted spears slammed into his shield and stabbed the ground all around him. Ty held his ground as hard as he could as their mighty attack smashed against his shield. But the ground was too soft, and he slowly started to slide back from the constant pounding from each hit he took. With the strength Ty had never felt before, he dug his feet in deeper and held his shoulder tighter to his shield. After the last arrow fell, he slowly stood up and lowered his shield to his side. "There are no weapons that can defeat me and no warrior that can conquer me! So let my friends go now or I will tear this place to the ground!"

That was when he felt the ground starting to shake and rumble. Bursting out from the steel cages that lined the streets and dark alleys came twelve blood-covered cave rats, snarling and chomping their razor-sharp teeth. Each one of them was as big as a full-grown saber tooth jackal, with metal spikes on their collars and armor tied to their backs.

In a split second, Ty reached back, grabbed four arrows, and sent them all sailing through the air like rockets. They whistled through the iron gates and plunged deep into those charging monsters. Then as fast as he could, he fired four more and slammed them through the hearts of four more charging beasts as they slammed through the gates. But there were four left, and Ty didn't have enough time to fire another shot as they hopped over the rats still twitching on the ground and through the gates, charging at full speed!

With the strength of ten men, Ty bashed one away with his shield and grabbed the second one by its tail; then spinning as fast as he could, Ty threw it across the courtyard and into an open window where a dozen Norgon warriors were hiding ready to fire their arrows again!

You could hear their screams as a battle erupted inside the room. The sounds of smashing timbers crashed through the air as Ty watched one Norgon trying to crawl out of the window, only to be viciously dragged back in again.

But Ty didn't have a second to waste as the two remaining rats ran through the thick field of arrows wedged deep in the ground surrounding Ty. The smaller one of the two was fast and nimble. It hopped and scurried through the maze and was about to pounce when Ty picked up a spear and ended its bloodthirsty attack.

Just as that beast hit the ground, the last vicious cave rat pounced. Ty dove out of the way as its teeth chomped down just inches from his throat. Then as Ty turned around and leaped to his feet, he drew his sword and sliced it in half, leaving its body twitching in a pool of its own blood.

With his muscles pulsing with courage, Ty turned around and faced the cold and dark city again. He looked around, then lowered his shield and slid his sword back under his belt. A small bead of sweat dripped down his cheek as he stood there watching the hordes of Norgon warriors scurry in the shadows in their war-torn armor, clanging and rattling their swords in a fit of rage.

Just when he was sure that legions of warriors were going to charge out from every direction, a thunderous sound burst out from the darkness—the deep and ominous sound of a horn that could make the souls of one hundred dead warriors shiver in their graves. Instantly, the clatter stopped and a silence fell over the area like a black mist.

Ty stood there watching as the streets became still and the city grew cold with silence. Then an old and bitter voice, crackling with rage, spoke out from deep within the shadows, "Who do you think you are to enter my domain? And why should I give you anything that my hunting party has captured?"

"I'm not going anywhere without my friends," Ty roared back. "If you want to live long enough to have your next meal, you better bring them back to me unharmed, or the next thing you'll find filling your belly will be my sword!"

"If you are speaking of that Zintarian scum and that pathetic snake, I will not release them. Zintarians are our enemies and they all deserve to die! And for that other one, I plan to make that pitiable excuse for a vipercon my dinner tonight. Now if you do not wish to be my desert, you should leave here right now!"

"You must be hard of hearing. I said I'm not leaving here without them. Hand them over now, or I'll rip this place apart!"

"Who do you think you're talking to, you puny man-child? I am Drockmar, War Lord of the Norgons. You are nothing but a foolish and scrawny young creature."

"However, I do enjoy a little sport before I eat, so if you accept my challenge of combat, no harm will come to you. If you survive, you and your pets will go free, but if you lose, I will roast you alive and place your empty skull on my wall!"

"How many of your pathetic guards do I have to kill in this challenge of yours?"

"All you have to do is defeat another stranger to my land, and I will grant you your freedom."

"Sounds to me like I'll be doing you a favor! Now let me tell you something, Lord Drockmar! If I do this and you don't keep your end of the bargain, I will show you no mercy. You can count on that!" Ty shouted back with thunderous defiance.

"Then it is agreed! Now if you want some advice, I think you should hurry. Just follow the screams of your pets. That shouldn't be too difficult for you. I just ordered them to be chained together and thrown into the pit with the other outsider. I'm sure they'll be quite close real soon!"

Ty walked cautiously past the open field between the wall of their fortress and the buildings surrounding the city. As soon as he was sure their archers couldn't get a clear shot, he bolted down the dimly lit black streets that were lined with torches made from the skulls of their victims. As he got deeper into that rancid city, he quickly realized that Lord Drockmar wasn't lying at all. It didn't take long at all until he could hear the faint screams of his friends echoing in the distance.

Frantically trying to find his friends, Ty's blood started to boil as he smashed his way through the barricaded doors that blocked the road into the heart of the city.

"Normack! Torg! Where are you?" shouted Ty. His screams for his friends bounced off the buildings and fell to the ground unanswered. Ty started to panic. He raced faster and faster with his star crystal clenched in his hand and forgot about the dangers that lurked behind the closed doors. There was no stopping him now; Ty would fight an army if they stood in his way. As he closed into the center of that city, the scratching sounds of claws against stone from the scurrying shadows began to rip his hope from his chest.

Soon, the sounds of cheering and screaming started to fill the air; he knew he was getting close.

He stayed on that main road and headed toward the billowing smoke and flickering light coming from huge fires in the fields that surrounded the ruins of a gigantic stone building. Its walls were covered with decaying moss and large cracks ran up its ragged pillars. *This has to be the place*, Ty thought to himself.

Just as soon as he got closer, Ty spotted a huge section of its wall smashed to the ground and piles of stone rubble littering the streets in all directions. Ty started to grin because he knew he had found his way in. Without a second's hesitation, he shoved his star crystal into his pocket and burst across that open field with his shield in his hand and his sword held high. Dozens of Norgons, busy throwing chunks of twisted logs into the fires by its rusted iron gates, turned and screeched in panic as they scurried into the shattered cracks in the walls like cockroaches.

"That's right! You'd better hide!"

With an explosive burst of speed, he leaped onto the rubble and sprang to the top in a flash. The thunderous sound of thousands of Norgons' screeching cheers started to drive Ty into a rage. A roar of a pure determination burst out as Ty soared into action. Jumping from shattered boulder to ragged stone, he entered the colossal arena. The cold walls were no match for his incredible sword as he hacked his way through the tight openings and the crumbling walls that blocked his way.

The sound of rock popping as it splits apart echoed into the hallway as Ty kicked the last chunk out of his way. Ty stepped into the opening and stood there for a moment, then grabbed his shield. Looking around, he could see a small flicker of light coming from the far end of that hallway, cold and full of hate. Ty took off running as fast as he could as hordes of Norgons started crawling out from the rubble behind him. Ty never looked back as he ran to the end of the hallway, then down the slippery steps into the arena. Full of anger and not a drop of fear, Ty swung his shield and smashed his way through crowds of scratching and scurrying Norgons to the great field cut deep into the ground.

"Get out of my way or I'll slice you in half!" roared Ty as he ran down the steps of that ancient stadium.

"Torg! Normack! I'm coming!"

Hundreds of Norgon started crawling over one another and scurrying up the walls, trying to escape as he ran through the crowd to the bottom row, and dove out of the stands to the field below. With a tremendous thud, he hit the ground right next to his friends.

Rancid thick dust swirled all around as Ty stood there with his shield in his left hand and his sword in his right. Ty took one look around at that stadium full of screaming Norgons as they started chanting and fighting among themselves. With a grin on his face and without wasting another second, Ty spun around and sliced right through those chains that held his friends so tight.

"Get up right now, you two! I heard that we may have some company down here."

Torg crawled to his knees and pointed to the shadows. "I think you might be talking about him!"

Ty spun around strong and defiant with his sword held high, ready for a fight. That's when he spotted a huge figure lurking deep in the shadows. "Oh nuts, this is definitely not good!"

Normack shook the iron net off his back, then rose up high and strong. "Nice to see you again, fish feet. Do you have a plan? Or are you just winging it again?"

"I got a plan, Normack. And it's a … Well, we have to … I don't have time to explain it right now! I'll tell you later!"

Normack looked down and started to laugh. "You mean if we make it out alive, that's when you'll tell me what the plan is, right?"

"Yep, that sounds about right," Torg chuckled.

"Very funny, guys! We wouldn't be in this mess if you two didn't get yourselves caught!"

Torg walked over and stood by his side. "It doesn't matter how we got here. We're here now, and we're ready! So let's get this party started!"

With that, Ty turned and started to walk over to that figure lurking in the shadows. "Hey, I heard you got thrown down in here just like we did. So let's work together and get out of here. What do you say?"

All three of them just stood there silently, waiting for an answer as hordes of Norgons screamed and clamored in the stands above.

But it didn't take long until they got their answer. Those beady red eyes glowing in the shadows slowly started to move into the light; Ty stepped back, then held his ground. He couldn't believe his eyes. "Crap, guys, I think we're in trouble!"

"What is it?" asked Torg as he strained to see what was coming out of those shadows.

"Hey, Normack, guess who!"

"What do you mean guess who? What are you talking about? What do you see?"

Ty put his sword away and pointed over at the shadows. "Hey, Grog, it's been a long time. Hope you're not going to hold a grudge about that little swim we had!"

Grog stood there for a moment and then started to tremble with anger. You could feel the air crackle with tension as he remembered their last encounter.

Ty turned to Normack and whispered, "That stink pit of a marsh must have been deeper than I thought."

Then with a deafening growl, Grog smashed the ground with his powerful hands and charged as fast as he could right at them!

Suddenly, a loud roar echoed throughout the pit as thousands of Norgons screamed and cheered as they watched Grog's thunderous rampage.

"Looks like we have an audience," laughed Ty. "But this time, Grog isn't going to hurt us again!"

All three of them scattered as Grog charged in rage. They knew they were trapped and had no place to run. Ty grabbed his rope and tossed one end to Torg. "Grab the end and hold on tight. I have an idea, but you have to be as fast as lightning."

With a sinister grin on his face, Torg nodded his head. He was ready for whatever Ty had in mind.

Ty boldly stood up and shouted out loudly, "Grog we don't want to hurt you, but if it's a fight you want, just bring that boulder butt of yours right over here! Hey, Normack, here's my plan. When I yell now, I want you to grab ahold of Grog as tight as you can!"

"That's your plan? You're nuts! Don't you remember the last time we tried that?"

"Yeah, but this time I'm ready!"

Grog was furious and charged across the field like an avalanche.

"If this doesn't work, we won't have to worry about being someone's dinner! Because that thing is going to grind us into jelly!" shouted Torg. "We'll be the dessert!"

"Now that's the spirit!" shouted Ty as he smiled and picked up a big fistful of rancid dust, waiting to make his move. Just as Grog got close enough to pound him flat, he threw it in Grog's face and dove out of the way.

Grog roared out in agony as that stinging grit dug into his eyes. Thrashing his head and swinging his fists in every direction, he stumbled blindly past Ty and slammed headfirst into the wall.

The crowd screeched and clambered for safety as the great impact split the stands apart.

"Now that's gotta hurt!" giggled Normack as he slid around behind Grog.

"Yep, I do think old boulder butt has made a good impression!" snickered Ty.

Torg looked over at Ty and threw the rope on the ground. "Would you two stop playing? All you're doing is making it madder!"

"I know! That's part of my plan! We've got to get him so mad that he'll want to smash us flat!"

"Well, its working! At least he'll kill us quick!" Torg snapped back in disbelief.

As Grog slowly squirmed and peeled himself out of that wall, he started pounding it furiously with all his might. Huge chunks of stone and dust started raining down on the crowd, smashing anything that couldn't escape. The sounds Norgons squealing in terror filled the air as they scattered for their lives.

Then Grog turned and stared with stone-cold fury and ripped a huge section of that crumbling wall, then sent it hurling across the field. *Kaboom!* A thunderous explosion rocked the stadium!

"Normack! Torg! Get ready!" shouted Ty as he ran to the middle of the field.

The rancid dust swirled across the ground like a storm cloud, then billowed across the stands. When it finally settled, Ty was standing with his shield in his grip and his head held high.

The crowd started to wail and cheer as Grog slung his arms out wide and roared like thunder. Then the ground started to tremble and shake as Grog blindly charged with a glare of a thousand knives at Ty.

"Watch out, Ty!" screamed Torg as he watched Grog closing in.

"Get ready! Just a little closer. C'mon, Grog, let's see what you got!" Ty shouted with commanding determination.

Grog exploded across the field, sending shards of stone flying as each step pounded closer and closer. In seconds, he was so close there was nowhere to run. Ty couldn't avoid his punishing attack. Their eyes were locked on each other; you could just see a small bead of sweat rolling down Ty's forehead as Grog drew back his fist and threw a horrendous punch.

"Now, Normack, grab him now!" screamed Ty as he ducked behind his shield, taking a monstrous blow to the chest. *Boom!*

"No!" shouted Normack as he rocketed over and tackled Grog with a thunderous crash and rolled across the ground in a furious fight. Clouds of dust and splintered bones swirled across the ground as Normack fought with every ounce of strength he had! Within a few seconds, Normack whipped around Grog and was able to get a crushing grip as they slammed into the steep walls of that terrifying pit.

"Now, Torg, let's get him!" shouted Ty.

The Norgons were screeching in shock and anger as they threw rocks and bricks down on them as they sprung into action.

"Hurry up. I can't hold him much longer! He's starting to get free!"

They dove right on top of their twisting and twirling bodies and went to work, tumbling across the ground.

Torg flipped and squirmed, then spun all around as he tried to wrap him up as tight as he could; with Ty pulling and tugging, they were able to tie Grog's hands tight to his chest.

"We got him, Normack! We got him real good!" screamed Ty. "You can let him go now!"

Normack slithered around and flicked Grog against the ground with a great grin on his face. "Now that felt good!" smiled Normack as he remembered the beating he took before.

Grog struggled furiously, rolling back and forth, as that rope dug in deep and strained under the intense pressure. But the more he struggled, the tighter the rope got. As the dust started to settle, the Norgons cheering stopped and the three of them stood boldly next to Grog, exhausted and covered with bruises.

Torg leaned over and spit out a couple of teeth, then turned to Ty and whispered, "We better find our way out of here right now! I don't know how much longer that rope of yours is going to last."

Normack and Ty both looked down at Grog and knew he was right.

Then suddenly, a voice echoed from the halls far above the field. It was Drockmar.

"Well, puny little man-child, you put up a great fight. You've defeated that monster of stone. I will allow you and your pets to leave here alive."

"Oh, great and powerful Lord Drockmar," came a simpering voice whispering from behind him. "Look there at the man-child. That little one has the ring of Zintarian royalty! That one must not leave here alive!"

"You're right! Prepare the archers. That ring *will* be mine!" whispered Drockmar back to his minion.

"Puny little man-child!" Drockmar shouted once more. "Before I allow you to leave, you must return that ring to me! It's mine and I want it back! Then you and your pets can leave, and you must take that thing with you! Now if you don't think that's fair, then, archers, get ready!"

Torg tensed up and nervously looked around as he watched the Norgon archers charge to the walls with their bows held ready.

Normack arched up, then slid cautiously by Torg's side and asked in a nervous voice, "Did he just say take it with us?"

"Yeah, Normack, he did," he replied in disgust.

"Great! This day just keeps getting better and better!"

Ty stood boldly next to Grog, then lifted his sword in defiance. "This is my ring, and you'll never get your hands on it! Our deal was that you'd let us go if I defeated this creature! Now if one arrow falls to the ground, I swear to you, Lord Drockmar, I will cut this monster loose right now and let it rip this place apart!"

Torg looked over in shock, then muttered quietly, "Drockmar. Ty, did you just say Drockmar?"

"Yeah, he's the one that told me that he was going to kill you and Normack!"

"So he considers himself a lord now?" Then he looked around to make sure no Norgon could hear him as he mumbled into Ty's ear, "Ty, listen to me! If that's Drockmar up there, he'll never let us go with Queen Lylah's ring still on your finger! He *will* kill us!"

"Then we have no choice!"

So Ty took a deep breath, then turned to Normack and softly whispered into his ear. You could see Normack's eyes grow with fright at what Ty was saying. "Normack, it's the only way," whispered Ty as he turned around and knelt next to Grog.

"Listen, I have a proposition for you. I could either leave you in this pit all tied up for eternity, or I could untie you and we could fight these things together! I promise I'll even help you find your way back home! So what do you say? Do you want to stay here all tied up or not?"

Grog stopped thrashing back and forth on the ground. You could tell he was thinking it over.

"Ty, you've finally lost your mind!" whispered Normack. "If you untie him, he'll crush us flat!"

"Untie him? Ty, did I hear Normack just say you're going to untie that thing? Are you two nuts?"

"Listen, you two, if we try to escape, we won't make it five feet before we're pin cushions! I think Grog would like it better to get back home, than be stuck down here in this pit for the rest of his life. But if you have a better plan, please let's hear it."

Ty turned toward the shadows where Drockmar was and shouted back in defiance, "I know now that your word means nothing, but you had better understand this: if I see one of your warriors anywhere around us as we leave or smell the stench of a single cave rat tracking us, I'll come back here and tear this city to the ground!"

With a smirk on his face, Ty reached into his pocket and pulled out a piece of diamond that was stuck in the corner. Then he pulled his ring off and threw the diamond chunk as hard as he could into the stands far above. With one last glance at Normack, he raised his sword and cut Grog free with a powerful slice.

"You're free. Now let's get out of here!"

Grog ripped the rope off from around his waist, looked down on Ty, and smashed his mighty hands together with a horrendous crack. Torg and Normack took a small step backward and looked over at Ty, shaking their heads and ready for Grog to attack. You could feel the crackle in the air as they hoped Ty knew what he was doing.

(To tell you the truth, I think Ty was making it up as he went along!)

CHAPTER 16

Into The Depths Of Earth

As the dust settled around their feet, the one question nobody had an answer for was how to get out of that arena alive. The walls were too steep for Normack and so slippery even Torg couldn't get a solid grip.

Ty looked over at Grog with a sneaky grin on his face. "Looks like the only way we can get you back to your home land is if you bash these walls into dust. Are you ready?"

With a grunt and a twitch, he turned toward the wall that held them prisoners and then let out a deafening roar that ripped through the cavern like a bolt of lightning.

"Rip it to shreds, Grog!" shouted Ty as he drew his sword and got ready for battle.

Grog ran over and started pounding with all his might. The shock waves that rippled through the ground began to make those tremendous stone pillars rock and sway. The cheering turned into shrieks of fear as the sound of crashing of bodies echoed across the field like a wave of terror. The crowd scurried for their lives as he pounded with all his might!

"Fire!" screamed Drockmar. "Kill them all!"

"Get back here, Torg!" shouted Ty as he reached out and snatched Torg off his feet by his tail and tossed him to the ground. "Stay behind me!"

Ty grabbed his shield and dropped to one knee. His muscles glistened by the light of the torches as he held his shield high and strong, preparing for the worst.

"I've got your back!" barked out Normack as he coiled up around those two, turning himself into a living wall.

As Drockmar's archers drew their bows and fired as fast as they could, Ty braced himself for the unrelenting barrage. Those poisonous arrows started raining down from every direction, splintering and shattering against Normack's thick scales and Ty's incredible shield. But as hard as they tried, they couldn't find their mark as the building started to crumble and collapse.

Grog's tremendous punches and fists of rage started to blast the thick stone wall into dust, and as soon as the last chunk of the wall fell to the ground, he started pounding his way into the stands, thrashing wildly and sending the iron benches crashing into the scurrying crowds as he pounded his way out.

I guess even a rock monster like Grog looks forward to a little payback because as soon as he clobbered his way out of there, he charged down the first open street and started to level everything in sight

Normack raised his head over the rubble and destruction left behind, then looked back down. "I can't believe it. He did it! C'mon, guys, let's get out of here right now. The coast is clear!"

The three of them didn't waste any time at all as they bolted for the exit. Thick dust was still swirling as they climbed out of there and stood in the dusty wake of Grog's rampage.

Normack looked around in disbelief. "This place looks like a herd of rinogs just ran through with their tails on fire!"

"You're not kidding, Normack!" replied Torg. "Now if we don't get moving, those Norgon creeps are going to regroup and attack. They don't run scared for long, you know!"

Everybody knew they had to get out of Norgon city as fast as they could and somehow find their way out of that subterranean maze. Unfortunately, the cave Ty found earlier was way too skinny for Grog to fit through. They had to find another way out fast, and they didn't waste any time discussing which way to go. They just took off running over the piles of rubble left behind by Grog's smashing rage and never looked back.

The thumping and scratching sounds of cave rats scurrying through the smashed buildings sent chills through their bones as they hurdled over the remains of the devastated building and the splattered carts scattered across the roads.

Suddenly, the high-pitched sounds of arrows screaming through the air came rippling toward them again!

"Arrows!" shouted Torg. "Follow me!" Torg turned and grabbed Ty's arm, then turned and ducked inside the remains of a huge house with polished floors and golden drapes flowing down across its shattered windows.

Normack started to flick his tongue and taste the air around. "This place is empty. We're safe."

"What is this place?" Ty asked as he looked around at the polished walls and golden statues.

"I don't know," muttered Torg. "It looks like a king's palace in here!"

Suddenly, Torg spotted two ivory bows with golden strings perched high in a glass case above a stone wall.

"Check that out!" Torg shouted. "This must be Drockmar's place, and they must be Drockmar's royal bows up there! Now considering that thief stole my bow and threw me into a rotten pit to die, I think he owes me a new bow. So I'm going to take those two up there!"

Torg reached back and smashed that glass case with his fist, grabbed both of those bows, and said, "Hey, Ty, since there are two of them, we both can have a new bow, compliments of Drockmar!"

"Nice! Don't mind if I do!" laughed Ty as he took the bow from Torg and pulled back on its string to test its strength. "And grab a bunch of those arrows too. I'm about out anyway."

Normack spun around quickly and snapped at the both of them, "You two had better start moving it or we'll get captured again. But this time, I don't think we'll get so lucky!"

Torg and Ty jumped down and peeked through the curtains.

"Looks clear," whispered Torg. "Are you guys ready?"

"Ready or not, we got to go right now!" Normack hollered back nervously.

Ty slung that ivory bow over his shoulder, then walked over to the door. "Well then, let's get going!" Taking a deep breath, he whipped the door open and took off down the street with Torg and Normack right behind him.

As they ran through town, you could still spot a few Norgons scurrying between the buildings and hiding behind giant mounds of rubble. You could tell that they would attack in a second if they got half a chance. Their beady eyes seemed to glow in the dim torchlight as they watched from the safety their hiding places. Even the giant vampire bats were flying in circles overhead as if they were waiting for the Norgon to give the signal to attack.

"This place is way too creepy," shouted Ty. "I'll be glad when we get out of here!"

"You're not kidding," replied Normack as he glided over a statue of a Norgon riding high on the back of a two-headed cave rat. "This place gives me the creeps too!"

Those three didn't waste any time getting out of that place. They rocketed across town and caught up with Grog as he smashed through an old barricade at the edge of the city.

They kept up that swift pace, running for hours over bitter cold trails and slime covered paths until the Norgon city disappeared into the darkness. The cavern became quiet again; even Grog's thunderous footsteps that echoed off the walls seemed to calm down into a peaceful drumming rhythm.

When Torg turned around and saw that they weren't being chased, he stopped and shouted to everybody, "Hey, guys! Let's take a break for a minute. My feet hurt and I think we all can use a little rest."

They were finally safe; the Norgons were nowhere to be found. They must have given up, or at least they were too afraid to show their faces. Who could blame them? The four of them together made a powerful army all by themselves.

Still, they had traveled deep inside that cave, and their muscles were aching with exhaustion. With a sigh of relief, everybody agreed and sat down side by side, hanging their feet over the edge of a deep crevice in the floor.

Grog, on the other hand, just leaned up against the cave's wall, exhausted.

Ty looked back and chuckled a bit. "Hey! Would you look at that? It's no wonder we never saw him that day in the field. He just looks like another part of the cave. That's cool!"

Normack just smiled and shook his head. "All he has to do is stay still and no one would ever know he was there!"

The three of them sat there for a while and tossed a few rocks down the hole, trying to see who could find the deepest part and betting one another that their next shot would be the best.

"This reminds me of back home," Ty explained softly. "Me and Bob would just sit around and toss a few rocks down the pit when we were bored and the fish weren't biting."

"I think I saw your brother," Torg said. "Back at the school, there was a kid playing outside and he looked just like you."

"Hey, maybe. Bob was wearing a blue shirt and I think he was wearing shorts. Did you see him?"

"Shhhh," whispered Normack. "I think I heard something."

Everybody stopped and held their breath. The thought of the Norgons approaching made everyone expect the worst, and they started to prepare for battle!

"What is it?" whispered Ty. "I don't hear a thing!"

"It sounds like there's a river up ahead. I can hear the sound of rushing water coming from over there," Normack said as he motioned into the darkness. "There's always a way out of a cave if you follow where the water is going."

"Well, what are we waiting for?" said Ty. "Hey, Grog, get up. Normack heard something up ahead, and we think there might be a way out!"

It took a few moments, but Grog lumbered to his feet, then with a low rumbling grunt, he joined the others, trudging down that dark and narrow path.

Torg quietly lead the way through the treacherous cavern, trying his best not to slip on the slimy green moss growing thickly all over the ground. The air was getting heavy and musty as they got closer to that underground river. The soothing sounds of the gentle stream flowing through the cavern sent the feeling of peace through our young warriors.

Finally, the cavern's walls began to spread out wider as they approached the river's edge. It was almost like the gentle arms of your mother as she welcomes you home from a long day. The cave was glistening with every color of the rainbow from the light coming from a split in the cave wall across the water.

"Great job, Normack! You did it! You found a way out," Torg hollered as he slapped him on his back.

"Let's try to cross over there," Ty said as he pointed downstream. "The water doesn't look too deep, and it seems to be calmer over there!"

"Are you sure you can make it across the river, fish feet?" asked Normack. "I remember the last time you tried to cross some water, it almost killed you. If you want, you can hold on to me and I will help you across."

He knew that Normack had his safety in mind, so he didn't get upset at all when Normack offered to help him across. However, the water looked shallow enough, and Ty knew that he had to conquer his fear of water.

"Thanks anyway. I have to do this by myself. This water isn't deep at all. I'll be all right."

"I can't believe we're almost out of this underground maze," Normack shouted joyfully. "I can't wait to feel the warm sun on my back again!"

Normack, Torg, and Grog splashed their way across to the other side pretty quickly, but Ty was still a little nervous and he took his time crossing. He was in no hurry at all.

Normack and Grog made it across in no time at all. Then as soon as they made it to shore, they headed out of the cave to bask in the bright sunlight. Now Torg was just a few steps behind them, and as soon as he started to crawl out of the water, he looked over his shoulder at Ty—just in time to see something long and slithery swim up right behind him.

"Don't look now, Ty, but you're not alone in that water. There's something in there with you! Get out quick!"

When Ty spun around, he was amazed to see a beautiful girl with hair like golden silk swimming in circles around his legs. She seemed to be quite curious. I don't think that she had ever seen a boy before, or at least not a young boy with legs. She gently swam around Ty a few more times, then rolled over and smiled as if she was trying to say hello.

"Normack, get back in here! There's something in the water with Ty!"

Normack bolted back in and stopped on the distant shoreline, trying as hard as he could to see what was going on. Torg looked kind of nervous because he knew the dangers that lurked in these dark waters. After a few more ripples swirling around Ty, Torg got his first look at what was under the water.

"Normack, whatever you do, just stay right there and don't make any sudden moves," whispered Torg. "That thing swimming around Ty looks like a water witch!"

"What do you mean a water witch?"

"I'm not sure if it's a water witch or not. I hope I'm wrong because if that thing really is a water witch, Ty's in big trouble!"

"I'm not going to stand here and do nothing if he's in trouble!"

"Just listen for a second, you big idiot! Water witches are powerful sorceresses, and they will trap your soul in the depths of the freezing waters if you make them mad! So just stay still!" he scolded as loud as he could and still not be noticed.

"There's nothing we can do over here to help Ty. The only thing we can do is to wait for it to come out of the water, and when it does, I'll be ready," he whispered again.

The beautiful creature just stayed there, drifting back and forth in that crystal clear water, looking deeply into Ty's eyes. Then with a soft and gentle smile, she reached up and touched Ty's hand as the cool water dripped from her fingers, and she slowly rose up.

"Watch out, Ty, she is trying to cast a spell on you!" screamed Torg! Then with an earsplitting hiss, he sent an arrow straight for the heart of the witch.

"What are you doing?" screamed Ty! Then frantically, Ty dove in front of that poisonous arrow a split second before it hit that young creature. *Crack!* The impact of that arrow echoed off the cave's wall like a gunshot as it slammed into Ty's chest.

"What did you do?" screamed Normack. "You just shot Ty!"

Ty flew back and splashed into the cold dark waves of that unforgiving water, disappearing out of sight.

A hideous screech filled the air as the water witch turned around and saw Torg standing there with his bow in his hands. In a fit of rage, she exploded out of the water as lightning shot out of her fingertips.

The crackle of her powers burst across the cave, making the water boil and time stand still. Her eyes glowed with shock and anger as she stared at them frozen solid by her spell.

Once they were firmly in her grasp, she reached down into the cold water and pulled Ty up and held him gently in her arms as he started to cough up water and gasp for air. He looked into her eyes, and he could see her fear and pain as she held him tightly in her arms.

"I'm okay," coughed Ty as he drew another breath. "My armor saved me from the arrow, and you saved me from drowning. Thank you!"

She let out a sigh of relief, and then a gentle smile crossed her lips as she slowly helped Ty to his feet. But her attention quickly snapped back to Torg and Normack, still frozen solid on the distant shore. Her rage grew stronger and stronger as the water surrounding her started to swirl once again.

"What are you doing? They're my friends. Please don't hurt them! They thought I was in danger!"

"They deserve to die!" she spoke out with an eerie voice. "They tried to kill me and they almost killed you. So why do you now risk your life to save them?"

"They were only trying to protect me! But I swear if you try to kill them, you'll have to kill me first!" shouted Ty as he reached for his sword.

She turned to Ty and grabbed him by his neck and lifted him clear out of the water. "You are a strange young creature, willing to risk your life to protect me and then willing to die to protect them. Why do you risk your life so foolishly?"

"They were just wrong. They just didn't know," gasped Ty. "Just like you right now! You're making a mistake. Nobody deserves to die because of a mistake!"

"Then why did you enter my domain if you weren't trying to kill me like the others?"

Ty kicked and struggled, then gasped for another breath. "We weren't trying to hurt anything. We're just trying to escape from the Norgons! They captured my friends over there, and they were going to kill us. We were just trying to get away!"

The water witch looked stunned and surprised as she listened to Ty's words.

Then looking back at Normack and Torg, she nodded and gently put Ty back down and told him in a soothing soft whisper, "You are speaking the truth. I can see what you had done to free your friends in your thoughts, and you seek the crystal mountain."

"Yes, that's what I've been trying to tell you!"

Slowly, she slipped back into the water, her hair drifting gently in the waves. She swam around Ty and stood up once more. "Many have come before you and tried to steal my powers, but you are different. You risked your life to save mine! So I will grant you your wish. They will not be harmed, but they can never come back here ever again, for if they choose to return, I will not be so forgiving!"

Ty was so happy he started to giggle and reached out and gave her a great big hug. "Thank you! These are my friends, and I know that they would never hurt anyone unless I was really in danger!"

She backed away, swirled around Ty once more, then stood in front of him again. "Maybe they were right. Maybe I was thinking about keeping you for a while!" She laughed as she ran her fingers through his hair. "For your honesty, I will give you a gift. You will have the ability to hear the thoughts of those around you when your heart and mind are at peace."

"What do you mean? I'm not looking for anything. All I want is to get out of here before the Norgons come back!"

"If you do not accept my gift, then maybe I will just keep you for a while. Now remember this! Their thoughts will come to you like a whisper in a dream, but be warned. If you cannot control your anger, those voices will rage within you like a thousand screaming banshees!" she cackled as she rose up high.

"Hey! All I want is to go back with my friends!"

"But first, let me hold you!" she screeched out loud as she lunged forward and grabbed Ty's head with both bands. Her eyes turned black as she smiled and held him tightly.

"Let me go!" screamed Ty as he struggled to break free from her grasp.

A smile crossed her lips as sparks began to jump from her fingertips and slice through his body.

"Come to thee the sounds of silence!" she chanted as Ty's eyes started to roll to the back of his head. "Open your mind and catch the dream, winter's thoughts and summer's screams! Into your mind, the thoughts will race, with a whisper and then with haste! Showers of night and into your dreams, birds of flight and raven's screams!"

Then in an instant, the still water turned bitter cold and started to crackle and freeze all around them as pillars of sparkling green ice shot up from the hidden depths beneath their feet. She smiled once more, then gave him a gentle kiss and laughed as he started to wake up from that trance.

"What did you do to me?" he muttered, half frozen and confused.

"You'll see," she said with a sinister grin. "Or better yet, you'll know soon enough!"

Ty broke free from her grasp and ran for shore as the river burst into flames.

She spun around furiously once more, then smashed a pillar of ice with one strike of her hand. "Run, little one, run! But remember to listen with a still heart!"

The flames were as cold as a winter's night and felt like talons slashing across his chest. Then with a clap of her hands and a banshee's screech, she propelled Ty across the water, and he landed by the feet of Torg and Normack, still motionless, and covered in a thin layer of ice. You could hear her laughter fading into the darkness of the cavern as the water became calm again.

Moments later, Torg and Normack came out of her sick and twisted spell. When they looked down and saw Ty's frozen body lying by their feet, they gasped in fear.

CHAPTER 17

Darkness Falls With Death Nearby

Moments later, Ty woke up from his frozen slumber, staring up at Torg's and Normack's worried faces.

"Pick him up and let's get him into the sunlight where he can warm up," Normack said anxiously. "We have to get out of this place before that thing comes back!"

"Are you all right, Ty?" asked Torg nervously. "You're shivering so much I can hardly hold you up."

"I'll be alright. All I need is to get warm and find some willow bark. My head is pounding so hard I think it's going to explode!"

"Don't worry," whispered Normack. "This warm sunshine will make you feel a lot better. Just lie down on this warm smooth rock and I will stand guard and watch your back while Torg looks for some willow bark for your headache."

With that, Torg nodded and ran off into the woods as Normack made his way up the side of a steep hill next to the cave and kept a watchful eye for any danger while he rested below.

"Hey, Normack! Where's Grog?" shouted Ty. "I don't see him anywhere!"

"I don't know! The last time I saw him, he was walking out of that cavern and heading down that hill when the water witch appeared."

"Water witch? What are you talking about, Normack?" Ty asked as he struggled to sit up a little bit. "Everything seems a little fuzzy. I remember making my way across that river when everything went dark. Then the next thing I know, I was waking up on the ground next to you guys, half frozen. What in the world happened? And what do you mean about a water witch?"

Normack went back down the hill and coiled up next Ty. "Well, I don't know much about water witches, but Torg said he knew what she was right away. You see, when Torg spotted her swimming around you, he said that she was some kind of wicked witch."

"Normack, did you see her?"

"Yeah, but not until we were onshore."

"Well, what happened then?"

"That's when he said he was going to scare her so you could have enough time to get away. But that's when things got really weird."

"Now it's going to get weird! This whole thing is weird. Was she some kind of mermaid or something?"

"Ty, I told you. I don't know what she was, but as soon as he shot his arrow, everything sort of stopped! We couldn't move, and we couldn't make a sound. It was like I was awake but still dreaming. Then the next thing I know, you were on the ground at our feet looking like a popsicle and she was gone!

"Wow, I can't remember a thing. I'm just so cold, and I got the worst headache I've ever had!"

Normack moved closer to Ty to help him warm up, then looked back at the entrance of the cave. "Ty, I don't think it's a good idea to stick around here for very long! So as soon as you feel up to it, I suggest we get as far away from this place as we can!"

"You'll get no argument from me about that, rat breath," Ty snickered. "I want to get as far away from here as I can too. There's something about this place that makes me feel really nervous."

"Well, which way do you think we should go now?" asked Normack. "I got so turned around in those caves I have no idea how to get you back home!"

"I don't want to head back home right now," muttered Ty. "I want to help Torg find his way back home first. All he was supposed to do was to help me make it back home safely with those rubies. But it was my fault he followed me down that pit. So I guess it's my turn to see that he gets back safely this time."

Just then, Normack stood up and peered deeply into the woods, his muscles tightened and rippled beneath his scales. There was definitely something out there.

"I think Torg is coming back," Normack said in a low and reassuring voice. "I can hear some light footsteps approaching. I want to be sure first, so I'm going to hide behind those bushes at the edge of the clearing, and if it's not Torg, I will deal with it myself. Just lie back down and warm yourself. I'll take care of it!"

Normack slithered silently across the deep green grass and disappeared into the thick brush as he hid and waited for whatever was approaching. It didn't take any time at all until a dark figure started to appear, quietly pushing its way through a tangled web of vines clinging to the trees at the edge of the pasture.

Normack made his move. He slithered fast and silently to head off the intruder before it got to where Ty was lying. But before that shadowy figure could slip through the wall of vines, Normack rose up tall and ferociously, his long white fangs sparkled in the evening sun, ready to strike.

"It's Torg!" shouted Ty. "Normack, wait! It's Torg!"

But Normack was too far to hear Ty's weak cry to warn him.

Torg pulled back the vines and jumped through a small opening he made. But just as he started to stand up, he was shocked to see Normack right in front of him, ready to strike.

"What are you doing?" shouted Torg. "It's me. It's me, you big rat breath, snake in the grass, blind as a bat, idiot!"

Normack shook his head in disbelief. "What am I doing?" muttered Normack. "What in the world do you think you're doing running up through the brush like that? You were one flick of my tail from being my next meal. I've got half a mind to end this right here and now and teach you your last lesson in life, you little twerp. *Never* sneak up on a vipercon, especially me!"

"Sneaking? Who's sneaking? I was making more noise than a herd of glop stoppers in a forest full of dishes!" Torg screamed back.

"Hey, you two, stop all that yelling. I can't take it anymore. My head's pounding and I need some rest!" yelled Ty as he fell back against that smooth stone slab with a loud hollow thud.

They knew he was right, and the both of them headed back to where Ty was without saying another word to each other, except for a silent moment when they looked at each other and nodded as if to say they were sorry.

"You can relax now. I found a real old willow tree growing out from the edge of a cliff. I climbed all the way up to the top of that wobbly old tree and gathered as much sweet bark as I could. I hope this is enough," whispered Torg as he laid down a nice big pile of fresh bark next to Ty's side.

But Ty was so weak that he just smiled, reached over, laid his head on top of that soft pile of bark, and closed his weary eyes.

"Let's leave him be," whispered Normack. "He's too weak to move right now. He needs his rest and it's getting dark. Why don't you get some rest too, and I'll keep watch? Tomorrow is another day, and we are going to need all the rest we can get if we plan to find our way out of this side of the shadow woods!"

"You're right, let's all get some rest and start off fresh in the morning." Torg looked around and found himself a nice, cool, damp resting spot between two moss-covered boulders (just like the caverns he grew up in), then laid his head down to rest.

Normack slithered back into the tall green grass again, happy to watch over them. However, this time he kept his watchful eyes focused sharply into the ever-growing darkness. He was the perfect one to stand watch in the dead of night. He didn't need a speck of light to know what lurked around, and with the slightest flick of his tongue, he could taste the air for any hint of trouble. He understood all too well that when nighttime crept into the shadow forest, the beasts that dwelled there came out into the cover of darkness to feed.

What made matters ten times worse was the fact that they were still camped out at the mouth of the water witch's cavern. Even though the creatures kept their distance from this place in the light of day, in the dead of night, the evil that crept in the shadows were drawn to it with an unholy devotion.

DAVID WALKER

There were no stars out that night, no sounds of crickets in the fields; only the passing dim glow that escaped from one of the twin moons was able to slip between the clouds before it was swallowed up again by the cold night air.

Normack watched over Ty as he tossed and turned restlessly on that cold, hard stone. Minutes seemed like hours while Normack's heart started to fill with fear as he watched Ty moaning out in pain. Whatever had happened to him in the waters of that cavern was ripping him apart. Normack feared that he would not make it through the night, and the only thing he could do was to make sure nothing else happened to him. No matter what the cost.

Hours seemed like an eternity as he kept watch. The sound of the tall grass swaying in the gentle breeze had an unnatural and spooky rhythm. It was the same creepy sound that filled the air just before something evil would show its face. It was way too quiet. Normack had that uneasy feeling that they weren't alone.

Torg must have felt it too because when Normack glanced over at him, he could see Torg's eyes slowly opening as he reached for his bow. With a questioning nod, Torg silently crept to his feet and slid around the boulders. "I'll go up to the top of the boulders." He motioned with the tip of his bow as he disappeared into the shadows above.

The fields were chillingly quiet; Torg could still hear the faint sounds of the river gently churning softly within the witch's cavern beneath him. As a royal Zintarian guard, Torg was still bound to his oath to Queen Lylah to protect and defend Ty at all costs, but he didn't need to be reminded of the oath he took so long ago; he would gladly give his life to protect his friends. So he quietly slid out three arrows and gently placed them on the soft green moss by his side, then drew one more and readied his bow.

There they sat, prepared for a fight. The air seemed to tingle with danger as they strained into the darkness, looking, watching, and fearing for what might be coming.

Normack grew more impatient. He could feel the soft murmur of movement tickling his belly from somewhere, somewhere close, but he couldn't detect any trace of body heat or pick up on the scent

144

of any creature creeping nearby as he flicked his tongue in the cool night air.

Suddenly, Torg stood up and drew his bow. "Over there!" he whispered to Normack. "There's something moving around behind that tree. It's getting closer!"

Normack ducked down and slid over to where Torg was gesturing to. His scales tingled with the sensation of danger as he got closer. Just as he slid behind the small tree, something darted across Normack's back and dove back into the tall grass, but as soon as he spun around to attack, it was gone. Then another thing zipped past the tree, and as he frantically spun around again, there was nothing to strike at. It was gone. "Did you see that? What was it?" shouted Normack.

"I don't know. I can't see a thing. Wait … wait … there … Something moving over there." Torg fired his bow and sent an arrow screaming through the night. *Whack!* He hit his mark.

As Normack turned, ready to strike, his eyes filled with fear. "It's … its … wait! I don't believe it! It's a raptoid spider! Hey there, raptoids!" shouted Normack. "No wonder we didn't see anything. Those raptoids' bodies are as clear as glass, and they're totally invisible when they stand still. You can be sitting right next to one and you would never know it. So watch out!"

"The one you got was a young one. It's only about the size of your fist, and it's still wiggling around over here! That poison tip arrow you took from the Norgons has no effect on it."

"What are you talking about, Normack? What the heck is a raptoid?"

"Are you kidding me? Raptoid spiders are feared by everything that lives in the forest. Even though their young may be as small as a pebble, their bite is ten times deadlier than mine! They can grow to be as large as a desert cat with fangs three inches long and can kill a full-grown rinog with a single bite!"

Normack took one more look at the grass in the field swaying back and forth and shouted, "We got to get out of here now! The grass isn't moving because of the breeze. This field must be filled with thousands of those things, and the sun's coming up!"

"Well then, all we have to do is keep them back until they go back into the trees! You keep them back, and I'll shoot anything that gets by!"

"Torg, you don't understand! They can't survive in the sunlight, so they must be headed back to the cave, and Ty's lying right in their path. If they find him, they won't pass up a quick meal like that!"

"Hey, your scales are tough enough to protect you. But mine aren't and Ty doesn't even have any. We got to get Ty out of here right now!"

There was no time to waste. Torg snatched his stuff up and dove through the air, landing hard on the ground behind Ty with a thud. No sooner had he hit the ground than a big raptoid spider burst out of the tall grass. Its cold black eyes shined in the fading moonlight as it attacked!

Torg swung his bow and smacked it as hard as hard as he could. It flew through the air with a high-pitched squeal and splattered against the wall of the cavern.

"Ty, wake up!" shouted Torg. "Wake up, wake up!"

But Ty just lay there like a lifeless corpse. So he reached down and grabbed Ty's shield, then leaped over him and readied himself for the fight of his life.

You could hear the grass rippling as the swarm of raptoids scurried toward them. Torg let out a thunderous battle cry as the raptoids started to shoot out of the tall grass. Torg smirked in glee because he could still faintly make out their silhouettes as they approached, still covered with the morning dew off the grass. "Sweet!" mumbled Torg. "I can see you! C'mon, you little freaks! Come and get some."

He swung Ty's shield and slammed the first one so hard that it splattered like an egg, then spun around and slashed the next one in half, sending one side of its body bouncing off the boulder Ty was lying on and the other hitting the ground, twitching as its blue blood oozed out. "Three down, one thousand to go!"

Just then, a wave of raptoids burst out of the grass. Torg had no time to think, no time to call out for help as he raised Ty's shield and sword, then started slashing and pounding everything that moved. The air filled with the sounds of battle, the screeching of spiders, the crack of the shield, and the sound of Ty's sword slicing and hacking through wave after wave of those monsters. "Hurry up, Normack! I can't hold them back much longer!"

"I'm coming, I'm coming!" Normack cried out as he shot over the boulders next to Torg. "Grab him and jump on!"

Normack quickly coiled up, making a wall between them, and the wave of flesh-eating raptoids as Torg struggled to pick Ty up. Then using his tail, Normack frantically started swatting them back, desperately trying to give him enough time to grab Ty.

"Normack, Ty's not waking up! He's not moving at all."

"Just grab him and throw him over!"

"I've got him. Let's get out of here!" Torg shouted as he flung Ty's body over his shoulder.

"Now hold on tight. If you fall off, you'll be dead before you hit the ground!"

Normack rose up high to protect his precious cargo and took off through the deep grass."

"Just hang on. I'll get us out of here!"

"I'm trying, but Ty's slipping!"

Normack looked back in terror as he slid through the tall grass. The sounds of raptoids popping and squishing beneath Normack sent chills through Torg as he clung as hard as he could.

"We're almost there!" shouted Normack. "Just a little farther!"

With a last-chance burst, Normack shot into the safety of the forest as the sunlight broke through the trees and burnt the last of the raptoids to a smoldering crisp!

"We'll be okay now!" said Normack in exhausted relief. "Just stay on my back and hold on to Ty. I'll find us a safe place to rest."

CHAPTER 18

The Mysteries Of The
Shadow Forest Deepens

Normack silently slipped into the fading darkness until he came upon a small clearing next to a slow-moving stream.

"Are you two all right?" questioned Normack as he slowly turned and eased them safely to the ground.

"I'm okay, but Ty still feels really cold. He's not like us. He should be warm all the time!"

"I know that. We have to get him some help. Wait! Look over there next to the stream. If I'm not mistaken, they look like minlar tracks.

"Normack, I don't recognize these tracks. What's a minlar?"

"Minlars are very small creatures, kind of like half hawk and half elf. They're an honorable race and very wise. If these are minlar tracks, they might help. That is, if we can find them *and* if they believe that we are worth their help! Stay right here with Ty. It's worth a shot to see where these tracks go. I'll be back soon!"

"All right. Be careful. I'm going to gather some dry grass and cover him up to keep him warm."

"Good idea. Tuck him in real good!"

"I'd sing him a lullaby too if it would help!"

"No, don't. With a voice like yours, I'm sure it would kill him. Just look after him and I'll be back soon!"

"Whatever!"

All Torg could do now was sit around and wait for Normack to return. Of course, one thing about the Shadow Forest that'll never change is you're never really alone and no creature will ever turn up an easy meal. So Torg stood guard again, just as he would at the entrance to Zintar.

An hour went by and the warm sun was rising up higher from the east when Ty started to roll over and knocked off the warm grass blanket Torg had made for him.

"Hey, dude. Are you all right?" Torg asked as he ran up to his side. "Just lie down and rest some more. Normack went out to get you some help. We were worried about you! How do you feel? Is there anything I can do?"

"I'm okay," whispered Ty as he rubbed his head and slowly sat up. "I feel like I just got sucker punched in the head by Pete and Joe. Hey how did I get here? Torg, what's wrong with me? I feel a bit strange"

"That water witch did something to you and you were out cold all night long. We had to get you out of there fast, so we carried you out!"

Ty just sat there silently for a few more minutes, then grabbed his spear and used it to brace himself as he stood up. His legs were a bit wobbly, and he was still a bit weak. As he looked around, Ty still felt a bit stiff, so he arched his back to stretch out, then slowly turned his head to crack his neck.

"I'm still cold and really hungry. When Normack gets back, let's look around for something to eat!"

"Sounds real good to me!" Torg chuckled as he sat down next to Ty. "I'm so hungry I'll eat anything!"

"Yeah, me too."

They didn't have long to wait until Normack came back.

"Hey! You're awake! How do you feel, Ty? We were afraid you weren't going to make it!"

"I'm okay. I just want to get out of this place and find something to eat. What happened to you? It looks like you've gained a few pounds. Or did you eat already?"

"Very funny, fish feet. It just so happens that I did find a little morsel to fill my stomach while I was out. But don't worry, I still saved a little room for you!" Normack said jokingly as he looked down at Ty. "But if it's food you need, there is a field of ripe fruit and apples that can get stuck in your teeth just over that ridge. You remember, just like that apple that got stuck on my fangs!"

Ty smiled and started to laugh. "Yeah, I remember!"

Torg bent down and picked up Ty's shield, then smiled and said, "Well, if you feel up to some walking, let's head over to that field. Some fresh food sounds really good about now."

Ty nodded and smiled a little as he leaned on his spear.

"Oh yeah," Torg remarked as he walked past Ty. "Whatever happened to those tracks you were following?"

"I don't know. They just disappeared past an old tree. I guess whatever it was must have climbed up or flew away. Let's just grab our stuff and get to that field!"

Normack waited for both of them to gather their things, and when they were ready, he led the way through the forest to a clearing across the stream. "We can cross here. The water is shallow and safe."

"How much farther?" asked Torg.

"Not much," he responded as they splashed their way across the stream. "We have to get to the far side of that cliff up ahead. There's a crack in the wall big enough for us to fit through coming up. When we squeeze through there, then you'll see! The entrance is well hidden, and I don't think we'll have anything to worry about once we get inside."

"Are you kidding me?" snapped Ty. "I don't want to go inside another cave right now!"

"Don't worry, you're going to like it there. I guarantee it!"

After squeezing past thick bushes and then crawling over two large trees that must have fallen during a real big storm, Normack turned and went up to the side of the cliff. "There is an entrance around here somewhere."

They looked all around and pulled back some vines and finally spotted some thick bushes growing right in front of that entrance.

It had sharp thorns and twisted vines growing on the walls of the opening.

"How in the world did you find this place, Normack?" asked Torg.

"I could taste the cool fresh air coming out from behind the bushes, and the aroma of fresh fruit made my tongue tingle! You call yourself a Zintarian guard, how embarrassing. Can't you taste it with that puny little-forked tongue of yours?"

As they squeezed their way through the crack, they got their first look at that valley and stopped dead in their tracks. It was beautiful! Deep green grass flowed gracefully across the ground like a thick blanket, and the trees were filled with all kinds of delicious fruits and berries as far as their eyes could see. There were apples, peaches, honeydrops, and cherries. Strawberries and grapevines crawled wildly up the steep walls of the cliffs surrounding the valley. It was like the most beautiful garden you have ever seen.

"Nice job, Normack! This place is awesome!" Ty said, grinning from ear to ear.

Normack had a big grin on his face, too, as he watched them looking around. "You two go and enjoy yourselves. I'm going to coil up in the grass and warm myself while you two get something to eat!"

"Normack, this place is incredible! Hey, you've been up all night long. Why don't you try to get some rest too?" Torg replied. "It looks like you could use some downtime."

They both watched as he coiled up in the soft grass. Then as soon as he laid his head down to rest, they both ran into the valley like two starving school kids at recess. Running from tree to tree, feasting on the delicious fruits and berries, they headed deeper into the valley without ever looking back.

"Hey, Torg, you got to try these cherries! They're so sweet they taste better than the ones you get on top of an ice-cream Sunday at Uncle John's ice-cream shop. But don't tell him I said that. Okay?"

"I've never tasted so many different things! We don't have this type of food in Zintar. The closest thing we have to cherries are the sweet green grubs that live in the moss in the ceiling above crooked creek. They don't have seeds, but they're pretty fast and you do have to catch them. The worst part is, if you're not careful, you'll get stung in your mouth and your tongue will go numb for hours!"

"You eat grubs? That's gross. I'll never eat a grub no matter how hungry I am!"

"You don't know what you're missing. They might be hard to catch, but they are really good to eat."

"Stop it. Thinking about eating grubs is going to make me puke. Just have another cherry and forget about it."

Ty reached out and grabbed a handful of cherries and threw them at Torg's back. *Splat!* They hit him right in the back of his head, and that sticky juice started dripping down his neck.

"That's not funny, fish feet! Next time you throw cherries at me, make sure you hit me in my mouth!"

They both started laughing as they sat back in that tree, swinging their legs and plucking cherries.

"Ty, I'm so full I can't eat another bite."

"Me too. This is awesome!"

Ty was feeling much better now. His headache was gone and his belly was full. They stretched out in that tree, finally carefree and relaxed.

It didn't take long until they were fast asleep, but Ty wasn't asleep for very long before he woke up to the sound of a faint voice softly whispering.

"Who's there? Who said that? Hey, wake up. I think I heard something!"

"What is it?" Torg mumbled in a sleepy daze. "I didn't hear a thing!"

"I swear I just heard someone. But it was weird. It kind of sounded like someone said that they wanted to go swimming in … lava mud? Pretty weird and creepy, huh? I must have been having a nightmare!"

"Nightmare, are you kidding me? That sounds like a great dream. I was just thinking about taking a nice dip in a steaming pool of lava mud. It would be perfect right now."

"In lava? Are you nuts?"

"Not in real lava. I'm talking about lava mud! You know, that's the mud that bubbles up from the cracks around a stream of molten lava. It's so hot and smooth it takes all of your aches and pains away. You just have to watch out because sometimes lava will shoot up into those pools and, well, have you ever cooked an egg?"

"Dude, you're nuts! I'd never swim in mud. First, being boiled doesn't sound like much fun, and second, my mom gets mad when my clothes get dirty! I think she would skin me alive if I went and took a bath in mud!"

"Don't knock it until you tried it! Now why don't you just relax and go back to sleep? You had a rough night and you could use the rest!"

"Hey, I'm not tired anymore. I'm going to walk around awhile and check out this valley. I'll meet you over by Normack later."

"All right, but don't go too far. After what we've been through, I don't trust any place on the surface land anymore. I swear it's safer walking around the caves near Norgon city than it is up here," he grumbled.

Ty just smiled, then jumped down and headed off to explore the valley. As he got farther and farther away from where his friends were, he started thinking about Queen Lylah and everything Torg had done. He wanted to make sure he got back safely to his home and remembered how pleased she was with the handful of apples he gave her.

With a determined grin, Ty ran up to a willow tree that was growing next to a small pond and started snapping small twigs off its flowing branches. *This is going to be perfect*, he thought to himself. Then as soon as he had a big pile of fresh twigs, he sat down in the cool shade, stripped the leaves off, and started weaving them into baskets. Now Ty never made a basket before in his life, but his mom had some baskets around the house, and he figured that it couldn't be any harder than making a net for fishing. For hours he sat there, twisting and pulling those twigs as best as he could, he made two strong baskets with crooked handles on top. He was so proud of himself because they looked strong enough to hold a lot of fresh fruit for their long trip back.

With excitement bubbling inside, Ty jumped up, grabbed the baskets, and ran around the valley picking armful after armful of the best fruit he could find. He made sure that they weren't too ripe so they wouldn't spoil while they walked back. He picked apples and honeydrops, cherries, and sugar fruit. In fact, he picked so much that the baskets started to bulge out in the middle. But he wasn't finished yet. Nope! He got down on the ground and started crawling all around, picking up handfuls of seeds from every tree he could find. He filled his pockets until he couldn't put one more seed inside!

Ty could hardly contain his excitement. He snatched up his baskets and flew back to where he had left Torg in that cherry tree. But he was already gone, so Ty kept his stride and headed back to where they agreed to meet, just outside of the entrance, over by the clearing where Normack was resting. By the time he arrived, his legs were burning and his arms felt like bricks from carrying those heavy baskets across the valley. Normack and Torg didn't see him coming because they were sitting with their backs toward him, and it looked like they were just sitting there talking.

"Hey, guys, check out what I've got! I've got an awesome gift for Queen Lylah when we get back!"

"What are you talking about, Ty?" muttered Torg as he slowly turned his head.

"This! Check it out. I've picked enough fruit so your whole village can have a feast!"

Ty stopped right next to his friends and dropped his baskets by their feet.

Torg's mouth dropped open, and he couldn't say a word. He just sat there in shock and mumbling.

"What's wrong with him, Normack? I thought he would appreciate this."

"Looks like you finally found a way to shut him up. I think he is in shock."

Torg stood up and gazed in disbelief. "You wish to give this as a gift for my queen? I can't believe it! This is the most incredible thing anyone has ever offered to a Zintarian queen! Why would you do such a thing?"

"Are you kidding me? If it wasn't for you two, I would be dead and my home would have been destroyed. This is the least I could do. I'm just embarrassed that I can't do anything more!"

"Again, you honor me and my people. I am the one that is privileged to be by your side," Torg said in a stern and confident tone as he knelt on one knee in front of Ty.

"I am too!" whispered Normack as he lowered his head with respect.

"Would you two guys stop it and get up? I think you must have eaten some rotten fruit and got drunk or something. We're a team, and I just wanted to pay her back for letting you help me!"

Just then, Normack saw something out of the corner of his eyes approaching fast from behind Torg. But before he could even flinch, an old minlar flew up, spread its wings out wide, and landed on the stone just across from Torg. Its sharp claws latched onto that stone like steel clamps, sending small puffs of stone dust drifting up between its talons.

"I have been watching the three of you ever since you left Morella's cavern. My name is Shaw-Shee. Now why are you here?"

"My name is Tyler. This is Torg, guardian of Zintar, and this is Normack, the bravest vipercon that ever lived. Why have you been watching us?"

"No man-child has ever entered these woods. Your heart is pure, but you are still naive. I needed to see if you were worthy of the tasks ahead of you!"

"Normack, what is he talking about?"

"What do you mean, what is he talking about? What are you talking about? That minlar is just sitting there staring at us?"

"They cannot hear us. You have been given the gift of understanding by the water witch, Morella. I needed to know if you deserved such a gift. Now I ask again. Why are you here?"

"What is going on with Ty, Normack?" Torg questioned.

"I don't know. Ty, are you all right?"

"Shhhh, would you two be quiet? It's hard to hear him. I'll tell you in a minute."

Ty told him all about his adventure and why he returned, then asked him if he knew the way back to the Crystal Mountain.

"The path you seek is not far. Just past the valley is the edge of the great blue fields. You will find a faster and safer route if you travel through the caverns by the northern cliff's edge. But beware. Do not go in too deep. That is also the way back to Norgon city. Stay to the right at the great falls and you will find your way back. Good luck to you and your friends. We'll be watching!"

With that, Shaw-Shee spread his wings and flew straight up and out of sight.

"What in the world just happened?" snapped Normack. "It looked like you were in a trance!"

"I'm not sure. That minlar was talking to me. I mean, I could hear what it was thinking, and I could talk to him just like I'm talking to you right now, but we weren't really talking. It was like I knew what he wanted and we understood each other."

"What in the world are you babbling about?"

"I don't know. It doesn't make any sense! He said that I have the gift to understand the thoughts of all creatures, and the water witch, Morella, gave it to me. How does he know about the water witch?"

"Morella. That was Morella?" Torg spoke out loudly. "Listen to me. Legends say that Morella was cast out from the underworld for her trickery and for empowering others with her magic. If she shared her powers with you back in the cold waters, you have to be careful. Nothing good ever came from her mischief!"

"You must have been hit on the head harder than we thought," teased Normack. "That minlar was just sitting there. If you have the power to read thoughts, then what am I thinking?"

Ty stopped and looked over at Normack, but nothing came to mind. "I don't know, and I don't know what happened to me back there. But I swear he was talking to me. I'm not crazy!"

"Well then, great wizard. What did it say?" Normack asked with a sarcastic chuckle.

"He told me that he was watching us for a long time and we would find our way back to the blue fields if we go through the caverns by the northern cliff's edge. I don't know what to believe, guys, but what do we have to lose?"

Normack swayed up and looked over to Torg. "I say we go to the northern cliff's edge. We have nothing to lose, and I'm curious."

CHAPTER 19

Back Into The Darkness

Torg slapped Ty on the back, then grabbed both baskets. "I'll carry these gifts for you. I'm sure your parents would be proud!"

Ty started to blush and smiled a little; he did miss his family a lot. He thought about what his mom and dad would think about what he was doing and started to laugh a little, then a guilty smirk started to show through. "You have no idea, Torg. If my mom really knew where I was and what I was doing, she would have a fit! She gets nervous whenever I go fishing by myself. But if she knew we picked a fight against the Norgons and I went after by myself, I think she would explode! Then I would be grounded until I was ninety."

Normack busted out laughing. "The great Cobasfang, lord of the Shadow Forest, grounded for life! Locked in his bedroom until he's ninety! I could see you now, hanging out of your window, yelling at everybody that walked by, 'Hey, buddy, do you wanna play checkers? I've got some warm milk and cookies!'"

"Stop it, Normack. Don't listen to him. We know you wouldn't have warm milk. That would give you gas. There's nothing worse than a ninety-year-old Cobasfang farting in his bedroom!"

"Nice, really nice, guys. I was going to let you two sleep over for a couple years too! My mom makes great cookies. It wouldn't be so bad."

By the time they stopped teasing him, they were almost at the other side of the valley. The cool shade from the great cliffs gave them a refreshing break from the hot summer sun as they walked through the grass.

"This place is great. I love it here," said Ty with a soft smile. "I'd like to bring my brother here and try some fishing in that pond we passed with all those lily pads floating around. I bet you there's are a lot of huge fish swimming around just waiting to be caught! Hey, Torg, those baskets are pretty heavy. Pass one over. I can carry one for a while."

"No, it's okay. I got it, but do you mind if I use your spear so I could slide it through the handles and sling them across my shoulders?"

"No problem, that's a great idea. Here, catch!"

Torg spun around and snatched the spear as it zipped by his side.

"Dude, that was a little close!"

"Sorry!"

"This is going to work real well," said Torg as he slipped it through the handles. "We used to carry our packs like this when we were in training. My guardian master would make us run up and down the river's edge like this until one of us fell. Then he would make the rest of us pick him up and carry him too."

Normack looked over and shook his head. "That sounds like too much work!"

"Trust me, it was a lot of work. But it did make us strong." Then he reached down and snatched the baskets off the ground like it was nothing at all. Resting the spear across his strong broad shoulders with his arms outstretched to help balance it, Torg started marching again.

Everyone kept quiet for a while, just walking and enjoying the peacefulness of that valley. They had no worries since they didn't have to keep a lookout for danger, and Torg was smiling all the way. He was so proud of the gift he was carrying and was constantly looking around at the bounty of fruit all around. After a little while of walking along the northern's cliff's edge, he leaned over and nudged Ty with one of the baskets.

"You were right, Ty. I can see an entrance to a cavern up ahead, just where you said it would be, and it looks just wide enough for all of us to fit through."

Normack looked over and saw it too. "I guess the next time he says a little birdie told me, we got to listen, right, Torg?"

"Yeah, I guess so," he chuckled as he nudged Ty again.

As soon as they got there, Torg set the baskets down in the shade and peeked inside the cavern.

"This place smells like rat breath. I guess that's perfect for you, Normack, so why don't you go in first? And if you sense any danger at all, just turn around and come right back! We'll stay here and wait for you to check it out."

"No problem. That sounds like a good idea. I'll be back soon. You two get some rest."

Then he ducked his head and slowly slithered into the darkness.

Ty took off his sword and bow and tossed them down next to the baskets, then he slid down against the wall and started to bounce a couple of rocks off a stump nearby.

"What's wrong, Ty? You look a little down."

"I always thought the Shadow Forest would be more dangerous to walk around outside and in the open. But let's face it, we got into more trouble walking around in those nasty caves under the Crystal Mountain."

"Ty, you don't have to go. We'll be all right."

"That's not what I mean. I really do want to go back to Zintar with you. I guess I'm just tired of sneaking around and being attacked by rats!"

"I know what you mean. It never was like that before. The Norgon used to be peaceful and they left us alone. That was before Drockmar became in charge. Now all he wants to do is raid our villages and steal whatever he can!"

Ty just looked over and threw another rock. "He sounds a lot like a couple of bullies back at home. I hope one day someone will teach him a lesson he'll never forget."

As they rested, Ty started to hear Torg's thoughts. He knew that he was missing his people too and longed to feel the peacefulness of his home as well.

"Hey, Torg, do you mind if I ask you a question?"

"No, not at all."

"Where did you get that scar on your back?"

"I got that when a Norgon war party almost killed me. You see, every ten years, when the twin moons and the second planet line up, seven guardians are chosen to escort five elders to the forbidden shores of the great waters. That's where the elders can speak to the creator and ask for his blessings for peace and good fortune, and then the chosen high priest of the elders will receive the creator's guidance and wisdom."

"Wow, that sounds pretty cool!"

"It's one of the most dangerous journeys a Zintarian guard could do. You see, three years ago, I was chosen to lead the Zintarian guardians in protecting the elders on their quest. It is an honor to be chosen for this mission."

"You went to the end of the world! What was it like?"

"Like I said, it was real rough. We had to travel right through the heart of the Norgons' country and then past the land of the dead. Over there, the hot winds are filled with sulfur from the lava flows, but that wasn't too bad. The worst part was the cave rats. They were all over the place!"

"How did you get past them?"

"Well, we were armed to the teeth and used up a lot of arrows. They started to leave us alone and feed on the remains of their dead until, one day, they attacked and ripped our supply cart apart before we were able to stop them. They stole half of our food and destroyed all of our water buckets!"

"Why didn't you turn back?"

"We had a mission, and there was no turning back!"

"We traveled using half rations for three days until we made it to the forbidden shore and set up camp. I sent out two of my guardians to hunt and resupply our food. They were great hunters and did a fine job!"

"Torg, what did they get?"

He started to laugh a bit, then picked up a rock and skipped it across the ground at that stump too. "I don't have a clue what that thing was that they brought back. All I know is that it had six legs, some really long teeth, and it tasted real good!"

"How did you know it wasn't poisonous?"

"Simple. We gave it to the elders first!" chuckled Torg. "No, I'm kidding. We cooked it real good and played throw down, and the loser was our taste tester!"

"What's that?"

"It's a game we used to play. You get a board and draw a circle on it, then take one of the jewels out of your sword and spin it real fast. The last person that stays in the circle wins! We used to play it all the time when we were younger."

"That's sound fair, I guess," laughed Ty.

"Seven days passed as we stood guard on the sandy shores until the elders informed us that it was time to return. They did not speak to us anymore on the way back. I feared their prayers were not answered, and peace was not to be in our future."

"They wouldn't even talk to you?"

"No, they just walked back in silence. Every once in a while, one of the elders would chant a little, but that was about it."

"Then what happened?"

"As we entered the land of Norgon, a scout spotted us and sent word of our presence back to Lord Drockmar. He set up an ambush for us as we entered a narrow pass. He must have wanted us to suffer and train his army because he didn't send in his pack of cave rats to cut us apart. He sent in two legions of soldiers instead!

"One came in from in front of us, and one crept up from behind, except I was ready for his attack. I realized that it was too quiet on our return, so I had three of my guardians dress up like elders, then left the elders and two more guardians to follow behind us in case we were attacked. Scales and I lead the way when the attack happened. We had no chance. Their army came at us from both sides, swinging axes and clubs. I jumped up and sliced my way into their charging hoards. But there were too many!"

COBASFANG JUSTICE RETURNS

"What happened then? And how did you and Scales get away?"

"Well, that was when I felt a tremendous crash in my back as a Norgon tried to split me in half with an ax. I must have passed out, and they thought I was dead. When I woke up, I saw the faces of the elders helping me, and my guardians were untying Scales. He was tortured and left in a net nailed to the ground to be eaten alive by insects. We were the only ones that made it. My other guardians were killed and hacked apart by those monsters!"

"Torg, if you didn't split up like that, your elders would never have made through alive. I'm sorry to hear about your men, but it sounds like they were real heroes, risking their lives to protect others."

Just then, Torg snapped his head back toward the cavern's opening. "I think Normack is back. I can hear him coming now!"

"It's about time. He was gone a long time!"

Ty stood up and watched as his two great big green eyes slithered out from the shadows of the cave.

"Hey, Normack, remember the last time I watched you sneaking out of a cave at me like that? What took you so long?"

"That's right, little morsel, just stand right there!"

Ty started to laugh and gathered up his things. Then Torg walked over to the baskets and got ready too.

"Two little morsels, that sounds twice as nice!"

As Ty turned around, he saw him slithering out of the cave.

"Watch out, Torg!" screamed Ty. "That's not Normack!"

Torg wasn't ready for a fight. He was just trying to sling the baskets of fruit over his shoulders as the vipercon snatched him off the ground. The baskets went flying as the fruit littered the grass below.

In an instant, Torg spun the spear around his head and slammed its point deep into the roof of its mouth, just as it struck!

"Bad choice for a meal, rat breath!" shouted Torg. "How does this spear taste?"

Torg held on tightly and jammed the spear in deeper and deeper as the vipercon's blood gushed out of its mouth.

"Hang on, Torg. I'm coming!"

Before Ty could even grab his sword, the vipercon started to shake and tremble as it lost its grip on life. The battle was already over. Torg had slain a vipercon!

"Torg, are you all right? You were incredible!"

"Help me get out of here, Ty. This thing is wrapped all around me!"

Ty pulled and tugged with all his might as Torg wiggled his way out of its cold dead grasp.

"No wonder why there aren't any rats around here. That cave must have been its home! But if that's its home, then where's Normack?"

"I don't know," Ty muttered. "Let's go and find out."

There was no time to waste. They picked up everything and took off into the cave.

Ty pulled out his star crystal and searched every dark slit in the walls of the cave, looking for any sign of Normack.

"He's not here. I don't see him anywhere. I think that thing let him go by just so it could sneak up and get us!"

"I think you're right. Normack must be somewhere up ahead at the other end of the cave."

Ty was right. As soon as they came to the end of the cave and into the huge cavern where the waterfall was, they found Normack lying on the shore of the river with a spear stuck in his side.

"What in the world happened, Normack? Are you all right?" Ty asked as he pulled out the spear.

"I'm okay. That toothpick can't pierce my scales. When I came out into the clearing, I was jumped on by a sneaky fat little scout. He was hiding behind those rocks by the water's edge and slammed that spear into me before I knew he was there!"

Torg looked all around and then looked back at Normack. "We got to get out of here right now before he reports back to anyone that we're here!"

"We don't have to worry about that," Normack hissed with a little smirk. "He's not going to snitch on anyone anymore. I just hope he doesn't give me a stomachache."

They both spun around and looked at Normack. There definitely was a lump on his side about the size of a Norgon.

"I guess that's one way to keep him quiet," laughed Torg. "But I prefer the old-fashion way with my spear."

Ty walked over by the falls raining down into the pool of clear water, splashed some water on his face, then cupped his hands and took a refreshing drink. "We got to go to the right and follow the river," he said as he pointed downstream. "Shaw-Shee told me that if we go any farther, we will end up back at Norgon city. I never want to see another Norgon as long as I live, so let's get moving."

"I'm with you. C'mon, Normack, since I'm carrying these baskets, how's about you take the lead again and Ty can cover our backs?"

Normack nodded his head and disappeared into the shadows along the river's edge. The sounds of the waterfall and splashing waters of the river hid the swishing sounds of Normack slithering across the sandy beach.

"Torg, we got to be careful. Shaw-Shee told me that this would be a shortcut, but Norgons did travel this way a lot. I'm going to use my bow and smooth out the sand behind us to cover our tracks."

"That's a great idea. You're starting to think like a true Zintarian guard. But don't make it too clean. A path that has no tracks is a path that will lead your enemy right to you. Do not forget that!"

"I won't. Did your guardian master teach you that?"

"Nope, Scales did."

The farther they went, the tighter and tighter the walls of that cavern started to close in. They were full of moss and wild poison berries that only grow in damp and musty caves.

"Hey, Torg, check this out! There's some drawing scratched in the wall behind that moss."

"You're right. It looks like some of the old scratchings we used to find near the lava pits when I was a kid."

"C'mon, let's keep going. The river's slowing down, and I think I can smell some fresh air!"

"I hope you're right. It would be nice to get out of here without running into any more Norgons."

"Just don't slow down and we will be out of here soon. I can definitely smell some fresh air trickling in."

Moments later, Torg stopped and started to smile. "Hey, Ty, I can see some light coming up ahead. We must be getting close."

"Not soon enough for me. I can't wait till I feel the warm sun again!"

"Torg, I'm not sure which way to go. The cave breaks off in two directions. Do you want to split up? You can take the right trail and I'll take the left?"

"I have a better idea. Grab one of those stones and throw it as hard as you can against the ceiling. Let me show you a trick."

Ty shrugged his shoulders and figured he had nothing to lose. So he did just what Torg asked. He picked up a good-sized rock and threw it as hard as he could. *Crack!* It hit the ceiling, splitting into three pieces.

Like an explosion of horror, thousands of vampire bats came streaming out of their hiding places right above their heads. Screeching and flapping, they took off like a massive cloud down the cave.

"Well, Ty, that's the way out. Just follow the screeching because I guarantee you, they are headed out of here as fast as they can fly!"

"Nice trick. I've got to remember that one! Hey look, there's Normack. Hey, Normack, we made it!"

"You were right, Ty," remarked Normack. "That cave led us to the edge of Grog's land, and I can see the blue fields from here. The thing is, it looks like we won't be able to get across from here. We'll have to head down into the ravine and go the long way around."

"Not today, Normack. I'm not walking around Grog's land anymore. You two can stay here. If I'm not back, well, just go the long way and I'll see you on the other side of life. Because I'm not going to let Grog push us around again!"

Ty boldly walked out of the cave and into the field of rocks and boulders straight into Grog's territory. "Hey, Grog!" shouted Ty. "Are you here? Come on out. Wake up, boulder butt."

The ground started to rumble under Ty's feet once more as Grog lumbered up, turned around, then stomped a jagged boulder into dust.

"Now look, Grog, if it wasn't for us, you would still be trapped in the Norgons' arena. We mean you no harm and only want to walk to the blue fields so we can get to the Crystal Mountain. If you want to fight, then we will fight, but I would rather ask for your permission. So what is it going to be? Will you let us pass?"

Grog stood there silently for a moment, then sat back down and rested. Ty could hear his thoughts more clearly than he ever heard anyone else's before. He knew that Grog appreciated being freed from the Norgon's pit, and he would give them his permission to cross.

"Thank you, Grog. If you ever need my help, I will come and stand by your side like you stood by ours!"

Grog nodded his head as if he understood every word, and he lay back down. There was no more anger in Grog's heart. He was calm and at peace.

"C'mon, guys, everything's okay. Grog is going to let us cross his land. He wanted to thank us for freeing him and he's just lay back down to get some sleep, so let's go!"

"Normack, that young man-child has more guts than any creature I know. I don't think anybody will ever believe me when I tell them what we just saw!"

"I know what you mean. I saw it and I still don't believe it!" laughed Normack. "Now let's get going before Grog gets up and changes his mind!"

"I'm with you, buddy," Torg said, then turned to Ty. "Hey, Ty, we'll be right there. I just have to grab your baskets."

"What do you mean my baskets? They're our baskets. Now c'mon and hurry up!"

Torg and Normack just looked at each other, then shook their heads and grinned. When they finally got to Ty, he was just sitting down, waiting and swinging his feet back and forth.

"Let's get out of here, Ty," Normack spoke in a soft, quiet voice. "I don't want Grog to get upset, so let's get going."

"Don't worry, he's fine. In fact, I'm sitting on his belly right now."

"You're sitting on what?" Torg shouted out in total surprise. "Did you just say you were sitting on Grog's stomach? Just sitting there swinging your legs like you were on some swing somewhere?"

"Yep, I told you that I talked to him, and he said he was glad that we helped him out. Don't worry about Grog. He's pretty cool. All he wants to do is chill out. He just gets upset when something messes with his sleep. So let's leave him alone and get back to Zintar."

Torg looked over at Normack and shrugged his shoulders.

"Let's get moving then. We can be back in an hour with a little luck."

"Now that's what I'm talking about!" Ty said as he slid down Grog's belly. "I'll see you later, Grog, and I hope you get some sleep." Then he turned and slapped Grog right on his belly as he walked away, heading for the blue fields with his friends.

CHAPTER 20

The Return To Zintar

The walk back through Grog's land to the blue fields went by faster than before. They all were bubbling with excitement as they realized their adventure was almost over.

Ty took the lead and started walking with his shoulders straight and his head held high as they made it to the grassy edge of the blue fields.

"We're finally back where we started, Normack!"

"You're right, and I think we must've walked completely around the Shadow Forest by now!"

"Hey, Torg," Ty exclaimed, "let me show you something."

"What is it?"

"Over there, next to that pillar is where I killed that life leech. Let's check it out! I wonder if there's anything left of it after it's been lying out here so long!"

"All right, let's go."

Torg was eager to check out the place that he had heard so much about, so when Ty started to pick up his pace, he was right behind him step by step. Normack, on the other hand, wasn't too anxious to see that life leech again. He wouldn't mind it a bit if he never saw another one of those things again for the rest of his life.

When they were about halfway there, Torg looked back and nodded to him to hurry up. "C'mon, slowpoke, I don't want to lose you now!"

"What are you talking about? You couldn't lose me if you tried! I could follow the scent of those smelly armpits of yours even if I was underwater and had a dead sludge tarpon strapped to my face!"

"Are you kidding me? A dead sludge tarpon strapped to your face would be an improvement!"

"Hey, sounds like you two should get married!

"Good idea, Ty. Let me wrap a ring around his neck!"

"Very funny, like you could afford one!"

Ty ran right up to the spot where he had killed that thing and looked all over. "Normack, it's gone! There's nothing left. Something must have come over here ate everything up!"

"You're right," Normack replied as he stopped next to Ty. "Whatever did that must have been really hungry!"

"Scavenger beetles," said Torg as he pointed at the loose dirt. "Look, no big tracks and the top layer of dirt is gone. Those things don't mess around when they strip a carcass clean. They take everything!"

Suddenly, Ty looked over at Normack and sat back down on the edge of the crystal. "I just remembered something. I don't think you can come with us to Zintar!"

Torg put the baskets down and put his hands on Ty's shoulders. "What are you talking about? He will be welcomed to my land!"

"I'm talking about the cave!" Ty snapped back as he threw a small piece of crystal across the ground. "Don't you remember? He'll never fit down the crack that leads to the river. He's too big!"

"Relax, Ty, I was thinking about that too, and there might be another way back!"

"Where? We looked all over this mountain, and that was the only cave that led into the underground tunnels!"

"Don't you remember when Scales and I climbed up the far side of the cliff? I saw an old lava tube next to the wall behind where you were sitting. We can go down it and find another way back. Even if it goes all the way to the fire river, I'm sure I can get us back!"

Normack stood up and shook his head. "No, I'll stay out here again. I don't want you to take a dangerous path just so I can come along. It's more important to get Torg back safely with your gifts."

"Would you two trust me? I'd rather go back that way anyway. Going back the way we came in would be too dangerous. Norgon hunting parties go there a lot, so the lava tube would be a lot safer."

"All right then," Ty said as he stood up and slung his bow over his shoulder. "Let's get going!"

Ty jumped down and took the lead while Torg was adjusting the baskets on the spear. "Don't wait for me. I'm right behind you!"

It was a real short trip back to the hidden entrance Ty had found so long ago. The splintered branches were still scattered across the ground where he chopped his way through. "We made it, guys!" screamed Ty as he darted through the brush. "C'mon, were almost there!"

Normack smiled and ducked his head as he glided through the opening. "So this is what that cavern looks like. The way you were talking about it, I thought it would have been smaller!"

"This is where we had our first run-in with that rinog," Ty explained as he showed him the slash marks on the crystal walls from their fight.

"With all these snapped arrows around, it looks like you guys had your hands full!"

"You're right about that," Torg said as he walked by both of them. "We were lucky to make it out of here alive. Now follow me and I'll show you the where that tunnel is."

Ty started to grin and ran up next to Torg as they approached the tunnel. "Hey, how about handing me one of those baskets please? There's no way you'll fit inside carrying them that way. Besides, I think it'll be easier if we drag the baskets. The tunnel is as smooth as glass, and if we tie my rope around them, we can pull them behind us."

"Listen to him, Torg. He's making a lot of sense. It would be a lot easier that way."

"All right then. Toss me an end and I'll tie it off."

Seconds later, Torg had his basket secured and started to head down the tunnel with Ty close behind. However, Normack stayed back a little just in case the tunnel became too narrow, so he could turn around and not get stuck.

The tunnel was perfectly round, and every little sound seemed to ping off its walls like a marble in a glass as they cautiously made their way back into Torg's land. It was the easiest path they had ever taken.

While they traveled, Torg explained that the tunnel was created millions of years ago when lava burned its way through the rock and helped create the crystal mountain.

"I have been in a tunnel like this before," Normack softly said from behind. "We have to be really careful. The ground always seems strong, but it could shatter at any time. I chased a proglidon down one of these tunnels before, and it fell through the floor before I could catch it."

"They could get pretty big. How big was it?" Torg asked.

"It was a good-sized one and would have made a good meal, about the size of a bull sloth, I guess."

"Well, I don't think we have to worry about that, Normack. They weigh a lot more than we do, and they stomp hard when they walk."

Ty looked back and didn't say a word. The scratching sounds of the baskets dragging across the ground made it a little hard to hear what everyone was saying. So everyone just kept on going and enjoyed the smooth path they chose.

"We must be getting closer to the great fire river," Torg finally pointed out. "I can feel the heat and the air is getting dry."

"Is that close to Zintar?" Ty asked.

"Yeah, not far at all. There's a tunnel there that'll lead us to the far side of the gates of Zintar. The only problem will be crossing the river."

"Wait, you didn't say anything about crossing a river of fire, and I'm guessing you're talking about a river of lava," snapped Ty.

"Don't worry about it until we get there. It all depends on how fast it's flowing. On a good day, when it flows soft and slow, there is a bridge we can use to get across, but when the river is angry, the fire is too close and we'll just have to find another way around."

"Sounds a bit dangerous to me. You guys say I take too many chances!" he chuckled as he looked back at Normack.

"Looks to me like Ty's rubbing off on you a little bit, Torg. I hope you know what you're doing."

"I know what I'm doing! You see, I told you I know what I was doing. The fire river is right up ahead. I can see the red glow from here!"

"You're right, I can see it too. Hey, Normack, wait till you see it. There's a huge cavern up ahead that looks like it's covered in black glass. The whole place is glistening red and orange, and there's a huge river of lava flowing right down the middle!"

He hurried up and quickly caught up to them and lay down by their sides, amazed by the sheer beauty of the cavern.

"I've seen many tunnels and caverns in my life, but this one is the most magnificent one of them all! Now where is that bridge you were talking about?"

Torg turned and pointed downstream. "Down there, the cavern narrows where an ancient column fell across. We can cross there! And, Ty, let me have the basket back now. It'll be easier for me to keep my balance while we walk across the black glass if I carry them both."

Ty agreed and untied his basket, then coiled up his rope and slung it over his shoulder again.

"Be very careful!" warned Torg. "The ground is very slippery, and if you fall, you'll land in the river. I have lost two of my fellow guardians that way!"

The path along the river of fire was steep and slippery. Ty was using his spear to help him keep his balance while Torg struggled as the baskets swung back and forth. They made their way over slick boulders and hopped across large gaps in the path.

"Torg, wait up!" Ty finally spoke up. "I don't want you to slip and fall. Those baskets aren't worth it."

"I'll be okay! Just don't come too close. If I fall, I don't want to knock you over!"

"I've got an idea. Let me tie my rope around you, so if you fall, you won't land in the river!"

"Listen to him, Torg. Our young warrior is finally using his head! We've come too far together to lose you now."

173

"All right, just be careful!"

Ty tied him off as gently as he could and wrapped the other end around himself as tight as he could. "We're in this together now, so if you fall, remember to let go of the baskets, okay?"

Normack smiled as they continued across the river's edge. It was flowing softly, but the heat was almost unbearable even for a cold-blooded serpent like him.

"I can see the bridge from here!" shouted Torg. "We're almost there!"

"I can see it too, but look, it's missing a piece in the middle!"

"It was never like that before. Something must have happened!"

As they made their way to the bridge, they could see that there was a portion missing from the center. Its black glassy arch was wide and strong, and there was a section broken off in the center that was too wide to jump over.

"We have to find another way around," Ty said disappointedly. "We can't risk crossing here!"

"We must try," Normack spoke out as he made his way up to those two. "This ground is too slippery, and I watched as you both almost fell countless times. I can make it past that small break, and you two can cross over me!"

"That's crazy! C'mon, Ty, let's keep going. I'll find us another way across!"

"No, he's right and you know it! He can do this and I trust him."

"I trust him too, but we have to be fast. The river can grow angry any minute and wash him off without warning!"

"Well, let's stop talking and get moving!"

Normack slid past them and slowly made his way across the bridge. The river sparked and flickered with orange fire as it flowed beneath him. Then as soon as he reached the gap, he coiled up and shot across without a second's hesitation. He wrapped around the other side as tightly as he could, then shouted out when he was ready, "Ty, you go first. You're the lightest, and when you get across, I want you to tie the rope off just in case I fall!"

"You got it" he replied as he started to crawl across Normack's powerful back. "I'll see you on the other side!"

He crawled as fast as he could, trying not to slip off his shiny hard scales.

"Hurry up, little one. It's starting to get a bit hot down here!"

Ty slid as fast as he could, then as soon as he made it safely across, he untied his rope from around his waist and threw it over a chunk of stone and held on tight.

"It's your turn now. Be careful!"

Torg dropped the baskets and told Ty to hold on for a second as he tied them up tightly. "We can pull them across together when I get to the other side!" he said in a stern voice.

"Hurry up, Torg. I'm burning up down here!"

Torg didn't waste another second. He knelt like a runner in a race, then used his sharp talons to scurry across his friend's back in a flash.

"Holy smokes, you're fast!" shouted Ty as he watched him zip across.

"C'mon, Normack, were both across. Let's go!"

Normack slowly started to unwind himself from the side of the bridge just as a crash rang out across the cavern.

"Hurry, Normack!" screamed Torg. "Something smashed into the river, and there's a wave of fire coming right at you!"

As he turned and looked, all he could see was a wall of glowing red lava streaking right for him. "Get out of here!" he shouted as he spun his way across the gap. "And get inside the cave where it's safe!"

Torg spun around and shoved Ty into the cave as Normack came rushing by.

"Get inside, you fool! You're going to get yourself killed!" Normack replied as Torg reached to untie the rope.

"I didn't carry it this far to watch it burn up in the river of fire!"

Just as the wall of lava boiled up high in the cavern, he snatched the rope off and shot for safety. "Pull with all your might!" shouted Torg as he tossed the end to Normack.

With every ounce of energy they had left, they snapped the rope as hard as they could and snatched it across the river as the wave of fire engulfed the bridge.

"You two are nuts!" Ty shouted as he picked himself off the floor. "You said I was crazy and didn't think things through. If either one of you ever says that about me again, I'll hit you with one of those apples!"

"That's a deal," snarled Torg as he crawled back to his feet. "These baskets are more precious than you could ever imagine. I wasn't going to let them burn up without a fight!"

"Well, Torg, lead the way," Normack said as he rose up and looked down the tunnel. "We have a gift to give, and I can't wait to see your queen's reaction."

"Then follow me."

All three walked proudly, side by side, with their heads held high, as they entered the land of Zintar. The tunnel was smooth and clean with fresh air sweeping through. They could see the dim light of the torches that lined the walls of the great gates flickering in the distance.

"Look, Torg, there's your home. We made it!" Ty said with an eager grin. "Thank you for everything!"

"It was my duty and my pleasure to stand by your side!"

Normack smiled as he watched them head into the cavern in front of the gates. His heart was full of pride as they slowly approached the century.

"Who goes there?" came a thunderous voice from on top of the wall.

"It is I, Torg Rockmar, royal Zintarian commander! I am escorting two royal guests of our Queen Lylah! Open the gates!"

"Show us your proof, Commander!" the guard snapped back in disbelief.

As Torg looked over at Ty, he stepped aside and bowed his head.

"I am Cobasfang, lord of the Shadow Forest, open your gates!" shouted Ty with pride and determination, then held up his fist and showed the guard his ring.

"Open the gates! The queen has visitors!" commanded the guard. "Sound the horns, and prepare the royal Zintarian guards for an escort!"

The thick iron gates creaked and popped as they swung wide against the tall stone walls. Torg stood tall with Normack by one side and Ty by his other. The sounds of the trumpets that blow for the arrival of royalty echoed across the land as the shadowy figures of the royal Zintarian guards approached.

"This is cool," Ty muttered as he looked over at Torg. "I feel like a king!"

He just smiled and put the baskets on the ground. "You two are our guests. Now follow me. The queen awaits your arrival."

As the escorts arrive, Torg looked up and saw his old friend approach. "Scales, good to see you again, my good friend. I cannot wait to tell you all about our journey!"

"Where have you been? We went back to search for you and you disappeared into the forest. I thought you were killed by that rinog!"

"We nearly were. It's a long story, but the blue fire rubies were delivered as commanded. This young man-child has the heart of a dragon beating in his chest!"

"And who is this with you over there?"

"This is Normack. He has traveled with us and fought by our side like a true warrior. He is my friend and a hero."

"Good to meet you, Normack. Commander Rockmar is a hard one to impress! Guardians, pick up their things and take them to the palace, and, Commander, if you would follow me, the queen is waiting for your arrival."

Ty turned and looked over at Normack as they marched through the courtyard. "Commander? I didn't know we had to salute him!"

"That would explain why he's always barking out orders all the time," Normack snickered.

"Hup, two, three, four," giggled Ty as they walked up the stairs of the great hall.

"Shhhh. You two are embarrassing me. You're acting like children!"

"Sorry, Daddy," snickered Ty as they walked through the golden doors of the queen's throne room.

As they entered, Queen Lylah was standing at the edge of a long and magnificent table with her royal court by her side.

"I have heard word about your travels from an acquaintance of yours. I am pleased to see that you have returned."

"Your Majesty," Torg spoke softly as he bowed down on one knee. "Cobasfang, lord of the Shadow Forest, has brought you a great gift in your honor."

"Well then, bring forth the gift and let me see."

"Bring in the basket," ordered the sentry at the door.

As the door swung open, two guards started marching down the red carpet, then placed the baskets gently in front of the queen.

Her eyes grew wide in shock as she witnessed the magnificent bounty that was laid before her.

"I have never seen so much of these delicacies before. Why have you brought me such an elaborate gift? Were the blue fire rubies enough for you?"

"The rubies you gave to me were plenty, Queen Lylah. I wish to offer these two small baskets to you and your people for sending Torg to help me. Without him, I would never have made it back to my home alive. He risked his life for me many times, and I wished to repay you for that."

"Step closer, Commander. For your honor and bravery, you have earned the respect and gratitude of the people of Zintar. Rise and be known from this day forward as high commander of the royal Zintarian guards!"

Torg looked over at his friends, shocked and surprised. His mouth was hanging open, and you could see his tail shaking nervously.

"Congratulations, Torg," Ty said softly as he bowed his head. "You have brought honor to your queen and your people."

"Let there be a feast for all Zintarians. We must celebrate the return of these three heroes!"

"Wait, Your Majesty. I have one more gift for your people," muttered Ty as he walked up to the edge of the table. "These are the seeds of the trees that produce the fruit we have brought to you. If you plant them and keep them watered, they will grow and supply your people with enough food to live well on." Then as he reached in his pocket, he spilled out mounds of seeds and scattered them across the table.

"All you need is some place that has a lot of light and good soil."

"This one is full of surprises, I see," smiled Queen Lylah.

"You have no idea," chuckled Normack as he stood by his side.

"Take them to the hall of light and do what he says," ordered the queen. "We have a lot to be grateful for today!"

Torg walked over to Ty and put both hands on his shoulders. "Thank you for what you have done for my people. I will never forget it!"

As they were walking out of the throne room, a lone sentry came running in.

"Queen Lylah," he shouted as he knelt to the floor. "We have captured a Norgon scout just outside of the gates. He says there's a legion approaching from the west and they're going to destroy your kingdom just like someone that wears your royal seal has destroyed theirs!"

Ty stopped, then slowly turned his head as the words of the sentry echoed across the room. The flickering light from the torches froze in silence as Ty gazed at Queen Lylah.

Taking a soft breath, Ty bowed his head, then slowly wrapped his fingers around the hilt of his sword. "Looks like Lord Drockmar needs to be taught another lesson," he whispered as a sneaky little grin crept from the corner of his mouth. The legend of Cobasfang will continue.

David Walker has a staggering imagination. He has lived with his wife of over 20 years, has 4 kids, 6 grandkids and a couple of dogs. Poppy Dave will take every opportunity to do some *Walking Dead* couch surfing instead of watching some lame new cartoons. The thing he loves the most is at bed time, asking the kids; present, past or future? Real or make-believe? With these two little words, his imagination will be unleashed, sending everyone spiraling into the heart of the mind-blowing realms of the incredible. So, what are you waiting for? Go grab some popcorn and join them as they venture into this treacherous world of the Shadow Forest.